HA! HA!

Very Funny

500+ Jokes, Riddles, & Puns

Compiled and Edited by

Tom Garrison

Address all inquiries to Tom Garrison at: tomgarrison98@yahoo.com.
Visit the *Ha! Ha! Very Funny* Facebook page at:
https://www.facebook.com/Ha-Ha-Very-Funny-103013027804635/?modal=admin_todo_tour
Your comments are welcome.

Independently Published
First Edition
St. George, Utah
Copyright 2019
ISBN 9781702590327

HA! HA!
Very Funny
500+ Jokes, Riddles, & Puns
Contents

Dedication   5

Introduction   6

The Art of Joke/Story Telling   11

Sources   16

Jokes

1   Animal Jokes   17

2   Bar Jokes   26

3   Blonde Jokes   28

4   Crime/Criminals/Police Jokes   36

5   Doctor/Medical Jokes   40

6   Don't Fit in Any Other Category Jokes   44

7   Ethnic Jokes   51

8   Food/Diet/Eating Jokes   54

9   Gross Jokes   58

10 Lawyer Jokes   59

11 Men/Women/Relationship Jokes   62

12 Old People Jokes   76

13 Political Jokes   86

14 Religious/God Jokes   98

15 Science/Technology Jokes   106

16 Sports/Exercise Jokes   108

17 Work/Jobs/Money Jokes   112

18 Young People Jokes   116

Other Books by Tom Garrison   121

Dedication

Someone needs to be the audience when I audition a joke. Who better than my wonderful wife, Deborah Looker. Not only is she a great first audience for my stories, puns, and riddles, she also is an accomplished editor. She has read with a critical eye every word in my five previous books, and this one. Thanks sweetie.

I also dedicate this joke book to the countless people who have screwed up their courage and told a joke in public—maybe to a small group of friends, or the person behind them while waiting in a slow moving line, or in front of a crowd of strangers. Good for you. You have spread a little humor and laughs in a world sorely in need of humor and laughs.

Introduction

We all share a similar experience: standing in a slow-moving line at the Department of Motor Vehicles, or Walmart, or at a popular restaurant. Most people find it the very definition of boring and a waste of time. However, with a bit of effort, you can turn this negative happening into an endorphin festival. How?

For decades, when stuck in a snail-paced line, I have taken direct action to transform a dreary time into a fun time. Speak to the person in proximity and tell them a simple joke.

What surpasses getting a perfect stranger to laugh at a corny joke? You brighten their day, even if for just a few seconds. I love doing that.

Or, be the life of a dull party by spinning a few jokes/tales. Is there a better sound in the universe than human beings sharing a laugh?

Why do this? Several reasons. First, putting yourself out there builds your confidence in public speaking. Hell, it strengthens confidence in general. I was shy as a kid. Hardly ever spoke in class through high school, even though I was a good student and almost always knew the answer.

In college, several professors took a liking to me and encouraged me to speak publicly/in class. I even took a class in public speaking. Gradually, I became comfortable with public speaking and began to develop as a joke/story teller. This trend continued and within a few years I was giving speeches before crowds of hundreds, twice running for public office (Santa Barbara, California City Council), being interviewed numerous times on television and radio, and generally expressing myself with confidence.

Secondly, joke telling and the resulting laughter (or groans) is great for your body and mind. Many studies clearly demonstrate that laughter:

1. **Laughter relaxes the whole body.** A good, hearty laugh relieves physical tension and stress, leaving your muscles relaxed for up to 45 minutes after.

2. **Laughter boosts the immune system.** Laughter decreases stress hormones and increases immune cells and infection-fighting antibodies, thus improving your resistance to disease.

3. **Laughter triggers the release of endorphins,** the body's natural feel-good chemicals. Endorphins promote an overall sense of well-being and can even temporarily relieve pain.

4. **Laughter protects the heart.** Laughter improves the function of blood vessels and increases blood flow, which can help protect you against a heart attack and other cardiovascular problems.

5. **Laughter burns calories.** Okay, so it's no replacement for going to the gym, but one study found that laughing for 10 to 15 minutes a day can burn approximately 40 calories—which could be enough to lose three or four pounds over the course of a year.

6. **Laughter lightens anger's heavy load**. Nothing diffuses anger and conflict faster than a shared laugh. Looking at the funny side can put problems into perspective and enable you to move on from confrontations without holding onto bitterness or resentment.

7. **Laughter may even help you to live longer.** A study in Norway found that people with a strong sense of humor outlived those who don't laugh as much. The difference was particularly notable for those battling cancer (Help Guide 2019).

In order to keep mentally and physically fit, I always laugh or at least chuckle at my own jokes.

Third, laughing helps you connect with other people. A couple of years ago I began telling a joke to tellers at my bank every time I had business there. Now, whenever I walk in, they expect me to tell them the latest joke. Of course, I do. Because of this, I feel, and I'm sure they also feel, a connection between us. Some of them have begun telling me jokes when I come in.

Finally, joke/story telling enhances creativity. I doubt I've ever told a story/joke exactly the same two times in a row. I tailor the joke to my audience—among my older friends, I make the characters in the joke old people. Quite often an audience member will comment or make a quip about my joke/story. You must be mentally agile to handle their words with a non-hurtful humorous reply.

Let's back up for a bit and examine jokes. So, what is a joke? We all have an intuitive understanding. What do the folks who study such things say?

A joke is a display of humor in which words are used within a specific and well-defined narrative structure to make people laugh and is not meant to be taken seriously. It takes the form of a story, usually with dialogue, and ends in a punchline. It is in the punchline that the audience becomes aware that the story contains a second, conflicting meaning. This can be done using a pun or other word play such as irony, a logical incompatibility, nonsense, or other means. Linguist Robert Hetzron offers the definition:

A joke is a short humorous piece of oral literature in which the funniness culminates in the final sentence, called the punchline... In fact, the main condition is that the tension should reach its highest level at the very end. No continuation relieving the tension should be added. As for its being "oral," it is true that jokes may appear printed, but when further transferred, there is no obligation to reproduce the text verbatim, as in the case of poetry (Wikipedia 2019A).

Jokes can differ in form. As noted above, most take the form of stories with a punchline. Very short jokes are one-liners. Some are literally one line long; but they can be a bit longer. A good one-liner is said to be pithy—concise and meaningful (Wikipedia 2019B). One of my favorites: "What do you call a boomerang that doesn't work? A stick."

Puns are another popular form of jokes. A pun, also called paronomasia, is a form of word play that exploits multiple meanings of a word/term, or of similar-sounding words, for an intended humorous or rhetorical effect (Wikipedia 2019C). How about a pun about puns? "A pun is not mature until full grown (groan)."

Closely related to one-liners and puns are riddles. In fact, many one-liners are riddles. A riddle is a question, or statement, put forth as a puzzle to be solved, often including a pun (Wikipedia 2019D). For example, "When is a door not a door? When it's ajar (a jar)." Ha, ha.

It seems as if joke/story telling is a thoroughly positive endeavor. Well, that depends. For example, I do not tell "naughty" jokes. What is a naughty joke? Under that category I place jokes that are overtly sexual or generally mean spirited.

Many jokes make fun of human foibles. But, playing off minor flaws or shortcomings in character or behavior is a world apart from a full-on attack of someone or a group. The former is almost always laughing *with* someone, sharing common human weaknesses. The latter is most often laughing *at* someone, and in the process diminishing them.

There are a couple of reasons for not telling naughty jokes. First, telling an off-color joke embarrasses me. I'm not a prude, but discretion is the better part of valor if one is considering talking about sex or racial controversaries to strangers. Do we really need to joke about penises or vaginas or the racial faults of black/white folks?

Secondly, unless you know your audience very well, a naughty joke may embarrass them. The point of joke telling is to create good feelings and laughter, not to make people feel uncomfortable or angry.

Most naughty jokes I've heard, and I've heard plenty, are not very funny. I think a very high percentage of the time the joke teller is more interested in shock value than in getting a laugh. The joke is a vehicle by which the joke teller can show how edgy/hip they are in a semi-acceptable manner. It is a way to focus attention on themselves, not the material, since the material is so often banal.

A naughty joke teller also relies on peer pressure to get a laugh. Upon hearing a naughty joke, even a bad one, most everyone will laugh/snicker a bit. Why? Because no one wants to be considered a prig, we all want to be "hip." Tell naughty jokes at your own risk. You may develop a reputation as an insensitive clod.

These are generalizations and, of course, there are exceptions such as telling a racy joke to a friend you know won't be offended or attending a comedy show which includes known naughty/edgy joke tellers. But as with all generalizations, most of the time they are true. Some forms of "humor" aren't appropriate. Use your best judgment to discern a good joke from a bad or hurtful one.

I include ethnic and "gross" jokes in this book. I believe none of the jokes in either category are demeaning or mean spirited. You may not agree. Know your audience and decide for yourself if a particular joke will be met with derision or laughter.

I'm obviously not a big fan of naughty jokes. Do I want to censor them? Hell no. I'm a strong supporter of the 1st Amendment (what joke/story teller isn't?). Let the naughty joke tellers rise or fall on their material.

Are you ready? There are 500+ (507 to be exact) jokes/stories, one-liners, puns, and riddles divided into 18 subject categories in this book. Screw up your courage and tell a joke to a stranger in an appropriate setting such as waiting in a slow line. Make it a habit to spend time with friends who make you laugh. And then return the favor by sharing funny stories/jokes with those around you.

If you find this task a bit disconcerting, please read (perhaps study) the next chapter in this book—The Art of Joke/Story Telling. It provides several tips to become an accomplished joke/story teller.

Did you hear the one about …?

References

Help Guide website. 2019. "Laughter is the Best Medicine." Last modified June 2019. https://www.helpguide.org/articles/mental-health/laughter-is-the-best-medicine.htm

Mayo Clinic website. 2019. "Stress relief from laughter? It's no joke." Last modified April 5, 2019. https://www.mayoclinic.org/healthy-lifestyle/stress-management/in-depth/stress-relief/art-20044456

Wikipedia website. 2019A. "Joke." Last modified June 20, 2019. https://en.wikipedia.org/wiki/Joke

Wikipedia website. 2019B. "One-line joke." Last modified June 15, 2019. https://en.wikipedia.org/wiki/One-line_joke

Wikipedia website. 2019C. "Pun." Last modified June 15, 2019. https://en.wikipedia.org/wiki/Pun

Wikipedia website. 2019D. "Riddle." Last modified June 28, 2019. https://en.wikipedia.org/wiki/Riddle

The Art of Joke/Story Telling

Sure, everyone can tell a joke. Most jokes are humorous short stories. We all tell stories. However, how many people elicit a response not only because of the joke, but because of their style and presentation?

Like many skills, joke telling is an art with some rules. Take drawing, for example. Anyone can draw stick figures and they may suffice for most uses. However, drawing with precision, flair, and creativity is much more than stick figures. The same with telling a joke/story. It can be bare bones and maybe work, or a Picasso of storytelling. Joke/story telling is simply effective communication.

I've laid out some important guidelines to improve your joke/story telling. You can ignore them to your own peril. But, following these guidelines will improve your ability to communicate in general and specifically when telling a story/joke.

Know the Material

When telling a joke/story you have heard or read, make sure to get basic information correct, especially the punchline. This is not as difficult as it seems. I memorize the punchline and an outline of the story leading to the punchline. I doubt if I have used the exact same wording—excepting one-liners, puns, and riddles—for a joke I have told many times. It doesn't matter if the story makes sense and leads to the punchline.

It is acceptable, even encouraged, to alter the joke to more effectively connect with your audience. Only change the details—location, types of people involved, names of the characters, etc.—if they are not essential to the meaning of the joke. If the joke includes animals, you probably don't want to alter it.

For example, I often change the location of a joke to wherever I am when telling the joke. Hence, most of my jokes, where the location is unimportant, are set in St. George, Utah. If the location is just background, this connects the jokes with the folks hearing it. However, if the location is important, say a joke set in heaven or hell, do not change it.

I also change the superficial attributes of the characters. Deb and I have led a monthly hiking club (cleverly called The Hiking Club) for more than two years. The group is mostly older folks and at our pre-hike gathering on the day of the hike I always tell a couple of jokes. Almost all the jokes feature older hikers. The jokes could originally be about almost anyone, but using old hikers connects me to the group.

Know Your Audience

Although seldom considered by novice joke tellers, knowing your audience is important. As mentioned in the Introduction, unless you know your audience very well, a naughty joke may embarrass them. The point of joke telling is to create good feelings and laughter, not to make people feel uncomfortable.

You should also have a feel for their demographics and range of knowledge. Older people probably won't get a joke reliant upon some current idiom popular with young folks. On the other hand, in terms of general knowledge, a joke about "I Dream of Jeannie" (a popular 1960s television comedy series; Wikipedia 2019A) will most likely draw blank stares from an audience of millennials.

Although it is very difficult to gauge, it helps if you have idea of the working vocabulary of your audience. One joke in this book depends entirely upon knowing what "plethora" means. (It means "a lot", an "overabundance.") If you feel your audience does not know the meaning, don't tell the joke—it embarrasses them and make you seem pretentious.

In general, try to fit the jokes to your audience. Every joke/story has a target—people, places, animals, ideas, relationships, etc. Relating the target to your audience is crucial—I love telling old people jokes to old people. It helps that I'm an old person.

Helping your audience stretch their minds a bit is great, but going too far beyond their limitations may backfire.

Engage Your Audience

I often start out a series of jokes with a one-liner or riddle such as: "Why was the skeleton afraid to cross the road?" Even if the answer is "I don't know," you have engaged your audience, made a connection with them. (Answer: "Because he didn't have any guts.")

Jokes/stories are more powerful if they juxtapose casual seriousness with exaggeration or surprise. Virtually all story jokes follow this rule. The joke teller begins the story, adds some details, and then ends with a surprise. For example:

> Three friends, a blonde, a redhead, and a brunette were lost in the desert. They wandered around and eventually found a ghost town. While examining the pitiful few contents of the buildings, they found a lamp. To get a better look, the redhead rubbed dirt and grime off the lamp. As she was

rubbing it a genie popped out of the lamp. The genie looked around and said, "Usually I grant three wishes to one person. However, since there are three of you, I will grant each of you one wish."

The redhead said, "I miss my family. I wish I was back home." Poof! She was gone. The brunette wished to be at home with her cats and dogs. Poof! She was gone. The blonde said, "Awwww, I miss my friends. I wish my friends were here."

Don't forget to make eye contact. If you audience is one other person, or a hundred, look at them. Show them you truly want to entertain them, if only for a few minutes.

Many people talk way too fast for effective joke/story telling, or even communication in general. Slow down your presentation and clearly enunciate your words. Nothing is worse that telling a joke that people don't get because the joke teller slurred their words. Have you ever heard a professional comedian who runs through his/her routine?

Finally, be there when joke/story telling. Don't be half-assed about communication. Show your enthusiasm, have fun. There are probably professional comics who appear, or perhaps are, distant from their audience. But I can't think of any. Most people who tell jokes for a living seems to really enjoy their work, often laughing at their own jokes (I certainly do).

Body Language

As my wife can tell you, I tend to be an enthusiastic speaker. I'd be mute if I could not use my hands while speaking.

Body language refers to the nonverbal signals that we use to communicate. According to experts, these nonverbal signals make up a huge part of daily communication. From our facial expressions to our body movements, the things we *don't* say can still convey volumes of information.

It has been suggested that body language may account for between 50 percent to 70 percent of all communication (Very Well Mind 2019).

When you see someone with their arms crossed in front of their chest, what do you think? I assume they are closed off, defensive, self-protective, maybe wary or scared. Compare that with a person who opens their arms to seemingly embrace the world. What is this nonverbal communication—welcome, join me, let's have a spot of fun.

If it does not come naturally, practice using positive and inviting body language. Open yourself. The most likely consequence is better communication.

Be Creative

Many times, I take a one-liner or short story/joke and weave a whole narrative it, giving context. Don't be afraid to be creative. Here is the short version I came across on the Internet:

> Two dogs and looking down at a bunch of ants. The dogs hear singing. "Just like me, they long to be … close to you. Rainy days and Mondays always get me down. We've only just begun…"
>
> One dog says to the other, "Crap. We've got carpenter ants."

And here is the longer, and I think more interesting, version that I created from the short version:

> A guy and gal are cleaning their house. The woman sees a line of ants on the floor. A faint sound seems to be emanating from the ant column. She bends down and hears, "Just like me, they long to be … close to you."
>
> She's not sure what is going on and calls for the guy. He comes over and they both kneel down close to the line of ants. It again sounds like singing, but different words. "Rainy days and Mondays always get me down…"
>
> They glance at each other and neither can believe it. The gal doesn't much like ants and suggests killing them. The singing stops and they stand up. But then the singing starts again, "We've only just begun…"
>
> The guy looks at the gal and says, "damn, we've got carpenter ants."

[Author's note: In the joke, the ants are singing verses from three hit songs by The Carpenters. In case you forgot, or never knew, The Carpenters were an American vocal and instrumental duo consisting of siblings Karen (1950–1983) and Richard Carpenter (b. 1946). They produced a distinct soft musical style, combining Karen's contralto vocals with Richard's arranging and composition skills. During their 14-year career from 1969 to the early

14

1980s, the Carpenters recorded ten albums, numerous singles, several television specials, and sold more than 90 million records worldwide (Wikipedia 2019B.)]

One creative tactic is the use of strategic pauses. Learn to recognize when a pause, a second or two or several seconds, builds anticipation.

> A very large grizzly bear walks into a tavern and stands at the bar. The bartender comes over and asks what he wants. The bear says, "I'd like a whisky and...............[long pause]....................................... coke." The bartender says sure and inquires, "Why the big pause (paws)?" The bear replies, "I don't know. I was just born with them."

I can't promise the reader they will become the next Robin Williams or Eddie Murphy of stand-up comedy. But, if you follow and practice the above rules, you will become better at communication in general and telling jokes/stories in particular. To paraphrase a famous joke:

> A would-be joke teller asks a well known comedian how to get to the famous Improv Comedy Club in Los Angeles. Without pause the comedian says, "Practice, practice, practice."

There are 500+ (507) jokes/stories, one-liners, puns, and riddles divided into 18 subject categories in this book. Memorize one joke a day, and you are set for about 1 ½ years. That should keep you amused, and amusing your friends, for a while. Have fun!

References

Lifehack website. 2019. "How to Tell a Funny Joke." Last modification unknown. https://www.lifehack.org/articles/communication/how-to-tell-a-funny-joke.html

Very Well Mind website. 2019. "Understanding Body Language and Facial Expressions." Last modified April 6, 2019. https://www.verywellmind.com/understand-body-language-and-facial-expressions-4147228

Wikipedia website. 2019A. "I Dream of Jeannie." Last modified June 8, 2019. https://en.wikipedia.org/wiki/I_Dream_of_Jeannie

Wikipedia website. 2019B. "The Carpenters." Last modified August 10, 2019. https://en.wikipedia.org/wiki/The_Carpenters

Sources

There are 507 jokes/stories, one-liners, riddles, and puns divided into 18 subject categories in this book.

I have always enjoyed telling jokes. I began collecting them, printing out emails from friends containing a joke, in the mid-1990s. In the last ten years or so, I started printing jokes found on Facebook, other online and print sources, and writing down jokes I was told. As such, I have no idea of the original source of most jokes in this book, other than they were readily available to the public with no hint of being copyrighted. Except for signature jokes by famous comedians, virtually no jokes I encountered are attributed to a single source. Many I have heard or read from multiple sources.

From my research, it seems as if a joke can be copyrighted, but they seldom are. Why? First, federal copyright laws protect the expression of ideas but not the ideas themselves. Thus, jokes, even similar ones, playing off the same idea would not be copyright infringement.

Secondly, a joke creator must demonstrate that the subsequent use of the joke was not an original and independent creation—not easy to do.

Third, under copyright law's Merger Doctrine, if there are limited ways to express an idea, the idea will merge with the expression of the idea and the expression will receive no copyright protection.

There are other fine points of joke copyright law. All make it very difficult to claim copyright infringement (Law Shelf 2019).

In those few cases where I do know a source, it is acknowledged. I have not knowingly used copyrighted jokes. I have no interest in infringing upon someone's copyright.

References

Law Shelf website. 2019. "Copyright Protection: Can a Joke be Copyrighted?" Last modification unknown. https://lawshelf.com/videos/entry/copyright-protection-can-a-joke-be-copyrighted

Chapter 1
Animal Jokes

One-Liners, Riddles, and Puns

I just saw a donkey cross the road. The really cool thing was that he looked both ways before crossing. What a smart ass.

Some alligators can grow up to 18 feet. But most only have four.

Optimism is going after Moby Dick in a rowboat. Fearlessness is taking the tartar sauce with you.

What do you call a cow that doesn't give milk? A milk dud? Wait, an udder failure.

Before the invention of the crowbar, crows had to do all their drinking at home.

What did the fish say when it hit a concrete wall? "Damn" (dam).

What did the buffalo say to his son when he left for college? Bye son (bison).

What if your dog only brings back the ball because he thinks you like throwing it?

Do female frogs croak? They do if you hold their little heads under water long enough.

What do you call a dinosaur with an extensive vocabulary? A thesaurus.

A vulture boards an airplane carrying two dead raccoons. The stewardess looks at him and says, "I'm sorry sir, one carrion (carry-on) per passenger.

If cats could text you back, they wouldn't.

Don't tell me what to do. You are not my cat.

How many dogs does it take to change a light bulb?

Golden Retriever: The sun is shining, the day is young, we've got our whole lives ahead of us and you're inside worrying about a stupid burned out light bulb?

Border Collie: Just one. And then I'll replace any wiring that's not up to code.

Dachshund: You know I can't reach that stupid lamp.

Rottweiler: Make me.

Boxer: Who cares? I can still play with my squeaky toys in the dark.

Labrador: Oh, me, me!!! Pleeeease let me change the light bulb. Can I? Can I? Pleeease, please.

German Shepherd: I'll change it as soon as I've led these people from the dark, check to make sure I haven't missed anyone, and make just one more perimeter patrol to see that no one has tried to take advantage of the situation.

Jack Russell Terrier: I'll just pop in a new bulb while I'm bouncing off the walls and furniture.

Old English Sheep Dog: Light bulb? I'm sorry, but I don't see a light bulb.

Pointer: I see it. There it is, right there.

Greyhound: It isn't moving, who cares?

Poodle: I'll just blow in the Border Collie's ear and he'll do it. By the time he finishes rewiring the house, my nails will be dry.

The Cat's answer: Dogs do not change light bulbs. Humans change light bulbs. So, the real question is: How long will it be before I can expect some light, some dinner, and a massage?

I dressed my dog as a cat. Now he won't come when I call him.

Why did the three little pigs leave home? Because their father was a big boar (bore).

What do you call a solitary shark? A lone (loan) shark.

Which dog keeps the best time? A watch dog.

Why is a fish easy to weigh? It has its own scales.

If a farmer has 17 sheep, and all but nine die, how many are left? Nine.

Why was the rabbit upset? She was having a bad hare (hair) day.

What happens when a frog parks in a no parking zone? It gets toad (towed) away.

What did the pony say when it had a sore throat? I'm a little horse (hoarse).

Why are teddy bears never hungry? Because they are always stuffed.

Why was the baby ant confused? Because all his uncles were ants (aunts).

Why do dragons sleep during the day? So they can fight nights (knights).

Why did Mickey Mouse take a trip into space? He wanted to find Pluto.

What kind of dinosaur could jump higher than a house? Any kind. A house can't jump.

Why was the dog afraid of the ocean? Because there was something fishy about it.

What goes dot-dot-croak, dot-dash-croak? Morse toad (code).

Do you know why chickens are not allowed in church? Because they use fowl (foul) language.

What's better than a talking dinosaur? A spelling bee.

What kind of a dog doesn't bark? A hush puppy.

Stories

A man went to the movies and was surprised to find a woman with a big collie dog sitting in front of him. During the movie, a comedy, the man was amazed that the dog laughed in all the right places.

After the movie, the man said to the woman, "Excuse me, but it is astounding that your dog enjoyed the movie so much."

"I'm really surprised myself," the woman replied, "He hated the book."

A duck, a skunk, and a deer went out for dinner at a nice St. George restaurant one night. They had a great meal (I believe the duck had foie gras—a luxury food product made of the liver of a duck or goose that has been especially fattened) and afterward were sitting around chatting and smoking big cigars. However, when it came time to pay, the skunk didn't have a scent (cent), the deer didn't have a buck, so they put the meal on the duck's bill.

A guy comes home feeling horrible. His dog greets him with a wagging tail. He sits down and tells his dog, "Man, what a bad day. Today I killed someone."

The dog rubs against the guy and says, "That's okay. Bad things happen. You know I still love you."

After a while, the dog leaves and the guy's cat walks over. He tells the cat that he feels awful because he killed someone today. The cat looks up with a wry smile and raises his paw for a high-five and says, "Far out man. So did I."

———————————

A man drives up to a country store. The store has a large wrap around porch with an old guy and a border collie playing checkers. The man gets out of his car, walks to the porch, and says, "That must be a really smart dog to play checkers."

The old guy looks up and says, "He's not that smart, I beat him three out of the first five games."

———————————

A guy is walking down the street with a crocodile and a chicken. It is a hot day and they are thirsty. All three go into a bar and jump upon bar stools. The bartender comes over, looks at the three of them and asks what they want. The guy orders a beer, the crocodile a martini, and the chicken a Mai Tai.

The bartender says, "Okay I'll serve you three. I served chickens before, but never a crocodile. I didn't know crocodiles could talk."

The guy leans over and whispers to the bartender, "The crocodile can't talk, the chicken is a ventriloquist."

———————————

A woman brought a very limp duck to the veterinarian. As she gently laid the duck on the examination table, the vet pulled out his stethoscope and listened to the bird's chest. After a moment or two, the vet shook his head and said, "I'm sorry, your duck, Cuddles, has passed over the rainbow bridge."

The distressed woman wailed, "Are you sure?"

"Yes, I'm sure. Your duck is dead," replied the vet.

"How can you be so sure," she protested. "You haven't done any testing or anything on him. He might just be in a coma or something."

The vet rolled his eyes, turned around, and left the room. He returned a couple of minutes later with a Labrador Retriever.

As the duck's owner looked on, the dog stood on his hind legs, put his front paws on the examination table, and sniffed the duck from top to bottom. The dog then looked up at the vet with sad eyes and shook his head.

The vet patted the Lab on the head and took it out of the room. A short time later he returned with a cat. The cat jumped on the table and delicately sniffed and closely looked at the bird. The cat finished and sat on his haunches, shook his head, and meowed softly. He then jumped down from the table and strolled out of the room.

The vet looked at the woman, "I regret to tell you, but as I said, this is most definitely, 100% certifiable, a dead duck."

The vet went to his office computer, did some quick keyboarding, and printed a bill, which he handed to the woman.

The woman, still in shock over the death of her pet duck, looks at the bill and cries out, "What, $150. $150 just to tell me my duck is dead."

The vet shrugged, "I'm sorry. If you had taken my word for it, the bill would be $25. But the Lab report and cat scan added another $125."

There was this dinosaur named Sara. She wanted to make a few bucks and thought about her marketable skills. She could sew well and decided to make and sell blouses to other dinosaurs. She started her business and needed a pity slogan to get the word out. She came up with "Try Sara's Tops." What kind of dinosaur was Sara? (Triceratops)

A German Shepherd, a Labrador Retriever, and an orange tabby cat have died at the same time. They go over the Rainbow Bridge and frolic around in a large field. Then, off in the distance, they see this big guy sitting in a large chair, a throne, and walk over to investigate. It turns out the guy is God.

They sit in front of God who wants to know what they believe in.

The German Shepherd says, "I believe in discipline, training, and loyalty to my dog and human pack."

"Good," says God, "Come and sit beside me. Labrador Retriever, what do you believe in?"

"I believe in having fun and protecting my human and dog family."

"Very good, come and sit by me," God said. Then he looks at the tabby cat and asks, "and my furry friend, what do you believe in?"

The cat looks up and says, "I believe you are sitting in my chair."

A monkey was sitting in a tree by a river smoking a joint when a lizard walks past, looks up, and says to the monkey, "Hey, monkey what are you doing?"

The monkey says, "Smoking a joint, come up and have a hit."

So, the lizard climbs up, sits by the monkey, and has a few puffs. After a while the lizard says his mouth is very dry and is going to get a drink from the river. Unfortunately, the lizard is so stoned that he falls into the river. The lizard is splashing around, a crocodile sees this and swims over to the lizard and helps him back to shore. "What is wrong with you?" the crocodile asks.

The lizard explains that he was sitting in a tree smoking a joint with a monkey, got really stoned, and fell into the river while trying to get a drink.

The crocodile is somewhat skeptical and says he is going to check out this joint smoking monkey. He finds the tree and looks up and says, "hey monkey."

The monkey looks down and says, "Damn, lizard, how much water did you drink?"

Fred, from a poor family, loved animals and wanted to help them. He worked his way through veterinary school by working nights as a taxidermist. Upon graduation, he decided he could combine his two vocations to better serve the needs of his patients and their owners, while doubling his practice, and, therefore, his income.

He opened his vet clinic with a sign on the door saying, "Dr. Smith, Veterinary Medicine and Taxidermy—Either way you get your dog back."

My wife, who does not like spiders, found one and told me to take it out instead of killing it. So, I took it out to the corner bar. We had a few drinks. The spider is a cool guy. It turns out he wants to be a web designer.

A guy and gal are cleaning their house. The woman sees a line of ants on the floor. A faint sound seems to be emanating from the ant column. She bends down and hears, "Just like me, they long to be … close to you."

She's not sure what is going on and calls for the guy. He comes over and they both kneel down close to the line of ants. It again sounds like singing, but different words. "Rainy days and Mondays always get me down…"

They glance at each other and neither can believe it. The gal doesn't much like ants and suggests killing them. The singing stops and they stand up. But then the singing starts again, "We've only just begun…"

The guy looks at the gal and says, "Damn, we've got carpenter ants."

A very large grizzly bear walks into a tavern and stands at the bar. The bartender comes over and asks what he wants. The bear says, "I'd like a whisky and..............[long pause].. coke." The bartender says sure and inquires, "Why the big pause (paws)?" The bear replies, "I don't know. I was just born with them."

A boyfriend and girlfriend decide to do something a little different, something they had never done—go horseback riding. They drove to the local stables and walked toward the office. On the exterior wall near the door to the office was a large sign that reads, "For fast riders, we have fast horses. For slow riders, we have slow horses. For those who have never ridden, we have horses that have never been ridden."

They decided to go swimming instead.

Fido and Kitty were hanging out in the living room, resting from a day of dog and cat antics. Fido asks Kitty, "You know that feeling when you do something bad and you can't focus on anything all day because you feel so terrible?" Kitty replied, "No."

A momma cat and her four kittens were walking along and suddenly a large collie dog approached them. While the kittens cowered, the momma cat let go with a series of loud barks scaring the dog away.

Turning to her kittens, the momma cat said, "You see how important it is to know a second language."

A well-dressed woman entered a pet store and headed straight for the bird department. The owner let her look around for a few minutes, then approached her. "Can I help you?" he asked.

"Yes," she said. "How much is the green bird in the top cage?"

"Five hundred dollars."

"Fine," she said. "I have my car outside. I'd like you to send me the bill."

"I can't do that lady," the owner replied. "You take the whole bird or nothing at all."

Steve was driving down a country road when suddenly a chicken darted into the road in front of him. He slammed on his brakes, but realized the chicken was speeding down the road at about 30 miles per hour. Intrigued, he tried to follow the bird, but couldn't catch up to the accelerating chicken. The chicken made a screeching turn into a farm and Steve followed. The chicken slowed down and Steve noticed, to his amazement, that it had three legs. The chicken joined a flock of other chickens, all of which had three legs.

The farmer heard Steve's car and came out of his house. Steve said, "Three legged chickens. That's amazing."

The farmer replied, "Yep, I breed them that way because I love drumsticks."

Steve was curious, "How does a three-legged chicken taste?"

The farmer smiled, "I dunno. Haven't been able to catch one."

Chapter 2
Bar Jokes

Stories

I was at this bar last night and the waitress screamed, "Anyone know CPR?" I said, "Hell, I know the entire alphabet." Everyone laughed, well except for the guy lying on the floor.

A pizza was walking down the street on a hot day and got thirsty. It was passing a bar, so the pizza walked in and hopped upon a bar stool. It asked the bartender for a cold beer—what is better with pizza than beer.

The bartender gives the pizza a long look and says, "Sorry, we don't serve food here."

Two guys, Bob and John, are sitting in a bar, drinking and chatting away. Bob notices that John has a very nice wristwatch. Bob says, "Nice watch. What kind is it?"

John replies, "It's a Cartier."

Bob pulls out a small notebook and pen and asks, "How do you spell that?"

John says, "T-H-A-T." "No," Bob says, "The name of the watch."

A jumper cable walked into a bar and hopped upon a bar stool. The bartender came over and asked what he wanted. The jumper cable said, "I'll have a draft beer."

The bartender said, "It is a bit unusual, but I'll serve you. Just don't start anything."

A guy walks into a bar, hops onto a stool, and sits a lump of asphalt on the stool next to him. The bartender walks over and asks what he wants. The guy points to himself and says, "A beer please." Then he points to the lump of asphalt and says, "And one for the road."

Two guys are sitting in a western bar chatting away. After a few drinks, the first guy tells the second, "I do love country, folk, and square dancing. I can't get enough of it. As a matter of fact, I was addicted to the hokey pokey. But I turned myself around. And that's what it's all about."

A psychiatrist was in the habit of stopping at a local bar after a day of treating patients. The daily routine never varied. The bartender would greet him with a friendly "Hello doc!" The doctor would pull up a stool and say, "The usual, please." And the bartender would serve the doctor his usual.

"The usual" in this case was pretty unusual. It was an odd drink the psychiatrist had learned about during a vacation in Jamaica years earlier. The drink was a daiquiri, an ordinary daiquiri except for the addition of a chunk of walnut. Because the doctor was such a good customer, the bartender kept a small supply of walnuts on hand.

One day the bartender noticed the walnut supply was exhausted. His psychiatrist customer was due in a few minutes. The bartender searched the premises and finally discovered a cache of hickory nuts left over from a party. He decided to substitute a chuck of hickory nut for walnut and hoped the doctor wouldn't notice the difference.

The doctor comes in, they go through their routine, and the bartender mixes a daiquiri with a chunk of hickory nut. He sat the glass in front of the psychiatrist and said, "Enjoy."

He surreptitiously watched as the doctor took a sip and a look of confusion crossed his face. Another sip, more confusion. The doctor put down the drink and waved to the bartender who came over and said, "Yes, doc?"

"I have a question for you," the doctor said. "Please tell the truth. Is this, or is this not a walnut daiquiri?"

"Afraid not," the bartender sheepishly replied. "Actually, it's a hickory, daiquiri, doc (hickory, dickory, dock)."

Chapter 3
Blonde Jokes

One-Liners, Riddles, and Puns

Why did the blonde climb the chain link fence? She wanted to see what was on the other side.

_____

What is the dream of every blonde? To be like Vanna White and actually learn the entire alphabet.

_____

What do you call 20 blondes in a freezer? Frosted flakes.

_____

Since it is "Talk Like a Pirate Day" "Arrrrggg" How much does it cost a blonde to pierce her ears? A buck-an-ear (buccaneer).

_____

Why did the blonde tiptoe past the medicine cabinet? She did not want to wake the sleeping pills.

_____

What do you call a brunette standing between two blondes? The translator.

_____

You know it is a blonde when she agrees to meet her date at the corner of "walk and don't walk."

_____

Why did the blonde get so excited about finishing a jigsaw puzzle in six months? Because the box said it was for "2 to 4 years."

_____

What did the blonde say after glimpsing a box of Cheerios? Oh my God, donut seeds.

_____

How do you confuse a blonde? Put her in a circle and tell her to sit in the corner.

_____

Why did the blonde bring a ladder to the bar? Someone told her the drinks were on the house.

Why couldn't the blonde dial 911? She couldn't find the 11.

Why did the blonde only have three kids? She heard every fourth child born in the world is Chinese.

What do you call a blonde that dyes her hair red? Artificial intelligence.

Why didn't the blonde tell the doctor she ate some glue? Because her lips were sealed.

A blonde woman is in the doctor's office. She says, "Doctor, I keep hearing a ringing sound." The doctor replies, "Then answer the phone."

Stories

A young blonde gal is in an upscale department store looking for alligator shoes. The shoe saleswoman repeatedly tells her they do not carry alligator shoes.

"Well, maybe I'll go out and catch my own alligator and get a pair of shoes for free," the blonde shouts as she stomps out of the store.

The saleswoman replied with a smile, "Okay, little lady, good luck with that."

The blonde headed off to a nearby swamp, determined to get an alligator.

Later that day, the saleswoman was driving home and passed the swamp. She glanced over and was amazed to see the blonde gal standing waist deep in the murky water, a large caliber rifle in hand.

The saleswoman stopped and stood on the bank of the swamp and watched a nine-foot gator swimming rapidly toward the blonde. With quick reflexes, the blonde took aim and shot the alligator. As it died, she grabbed its tail and hauled it onto the slippery bank.

Nearby were five dead gators. The saleswoman watched in amazement as the blonde examined the newly dead alligator. She heard the blonde scream in frustration, "Damn, this one's barefoot too!"

A blond was driving her car around town doing errands. She noticed that a red dashboard light came on saying she needed to change the oil. Being a responsible car owner, she immediately headed for the service center.

She arrived and told the service manager about the light. He checked and said, "Yes, you need an oil change. I looked up your car's records, you bought it here and have been in for service before, and you are also due for a tire rotation."

The blond, being no dummy, told him, "Okay, the oil change seems legitimate. But you are just trying to take advantage of me about the tire rotation because I'm a blond."

Taken aback, the service manager replied, "What? You need a tire rotation. The records clearly indicate that."

The blond retorted, "How dumb do you think I am? I don't need a tire rotation. The tires rotate every time I drive the car."

A woman was visiting her blonde friend who had adopted two new dogs and asked what their names were.

The blonde responded by saying that one was named Rolex and the other named Timex.

Rolling her eyes, her friend said, "Whoever heard of someone naming their dogs like that?"

"Hellooooo," answered the blonde. "They're watch dogs."

A blonde guy shouts frantically into the phone, "My wife is pregnant, and her contractions are only two minutes apart."

"Is this her first child?" the doctor asks.

"No," the guy yells, "this is her husband."

A blonde is overweight, so her doctor puts her on a diet. "I want you to eat regularly for two days, then skip a day, and repeat this procedure for two weeks. The next time I see you, you'll have lost at least five pounds."

When the blonde returns two weeks later, she's lost nearly 20 pounds.

"Why that's amazing!" the doctor says. "Did you follow my instructions?"

The blonde nods. "I'll tell you, though, I thought I was going to drop dead by the third day."

"From hunger, you mean?" asked the doctor.

"No," the blonde replied, "From all that skipping."

A blonde girl in her late teens, wanting to earn some money for the summer, decided to hire herself out as a "handy woman" and started canvassing a nearby wealth neighborhood.

She went to the front door of the first house and asked the owner if he had any odd jobs for her to do. "Well, I guess I could use someone to paint the porch. How much will you charge me?" he asked.

Delighted, the girl quickly responded, "How about $50?"

The man agreed and told her that the paint, brushes, and everything she would need were in the garage next to the car. The man's wife, upon hearing the conversation, said to her husband, "Does she realize that our porch goes all the way around the house?"

That's a bit cynical, isn't it?" he responded.

The wife replied, "You're right. I guess I'm starting to believe all those dumb blonde jokes."

A few hours later the blonde came to the door to collect her money.

"You're finished already?" the husband asked.

"Yes," the blonde replied. "and I even had paint left over so I gave it two coats."

Impressed, the man gave her the $50 and a $10 tip.

"Thank you," the blonde said. "And, by the way, it's not a porch (Porsche), it's an Audi."

A blonde guy is in the shower and his wife shouts, "Did you find the shampoo?"

The blonde answers, "Yes, but I'm not sure what to do. It's for dry hair and I just wet mine."

––––––––––

The other day I was getting into an elevator. As I entered, a lovely blonde already inside greeted me by saying, "T-G-I-F."

I smiled at her and replied, "S-H-I-T."

She looked at me, puzzled and said again, "T-G-I-F."

I acknowledged her remark once more by answering, "S-H-I-T."

The blonde was trying to be friendly, so she smiled a big smile and said, "T-G-I-F, Thank God It's Friday ... get it"

I answered back, "S-H-I-T ... Sorry Honey, It's Thursday."

––––––––––

A blonde called her boyfriend and said, "Please come over and help me. I have a killer jigsaw puzzle and I can't figure it out or how to get started."

Her boyfriend asked, "What is it supposed to be when it's finished?"

The blonde said, "According to the picture on the box, it is supposed to be a tiger."

The boyfriend decided to go over and help her with the puzzle. She let him in and showed him where she had the puzzle spread all over the table. He studied the pieces for a moment, looked at the box, and turned to her and said, "First of all, no matter what we do, we're not going to be able to assemble these pieces into anything resembling a tiger." He took her hand and said, "Second, I want you to relax. Let's have a nice cup of hot chocolate and then ..." He sighed, "Let's put all these frosted flakes back into the box."

––––––––––

A blonde gal and her redhead friend went to a bar for a drink after work. They sat on stools at the bar and watched the 6:00 o'clock news. A man was shown threatening to jump from a bridge. The blonde bet the redhead $50 that he wouldn't jump.

Sure enough, the man jumped, so the blonde gave the redhead $50. The redhead said, "I can't take this, you're my friend."

But the blonde insisted saying, "No. A bet's a bet."

Then the redhead said, "Listen, I have to say I saw this on the 5:00 o'clock news so I can't take your money. I knew he would jump."

The blonde replied, "Well, I also saw it earlier, but I didn't think he would jump again."

Three friends, a blonde, a redhead, and a brunette were lost in the desert. They wandered around and eventually found a ghost town. While examining the pitiful few contents of the buildings, they found a lamp. To get a better look, the redhead rubbed dirt and grime off the lamp. As she was rubbing it a genie popped out of the lamp. The genie looked around and said, "Usually I grant three wishes to one person. However, since there are three of you, I will grant each of you one wish."

The redhead said, "I miss my family. I wish I was back home." Poof! She was gone.

The brunette wished to be at home with her cats and dogs. Poof! She was gone.

The blonde said, "Awwww, I miss my friends. I wish my friends were here."

A blonde, a redhead, and a brunette were stranded on a deserted island. The nearest shore and rescue was 50 miles away. The redhead tried to swim to the other shore, she made it 15 miles and drowned. Next the brunette took a turn, swam 24 miles and drowned. Finally, the blonde got in the water. She swam 25 miles, got tired, and successfully swam back.

This blonde got sick and tired of all the blonde jokes. One evening she memorized all the state capitals. The next day some guy in her office started telling dumb blonde jokes. She interrupts him and states, "I'm tired of all these blonde jokes. I want you to know that this blonde went home last night and did something probably none of you could do. I memorized all the state capitals."

One of the guys, of course, said, "I don't believe you. What is the capital of Nevada?"

"N," the blonde answered.

A woman pulled into a crowded parking lot and rolled down the car window to make sure her Labrador Retriever had fresh air. The Lab was stretched out on the back seat, and the woman wanted to impress upon the dog that he should remain there.

The woman got out of the car and emphatically said, "Now you stay. Do you hear me? Stay. Stay."

A guy in a nearby car waiting for a parking spot and noticing that the woman was blonde, rolled down his window and said, "Why don't you just put it in park?"

A blonde woman was speeding down the road and was pulled over by a female police officer, who also happened to be blonde.

The blonde cop asked to see the blonde driver's license. The driver dug through her purse, couldn't find her license, and was getting progressively more agitated.

"What does it look like?" she asked.

The policewoman replied, "It's rectangular and has your photo on it."

The driver finally found a small rectangular mirror in her purse, looked at it, and handed it to the policewoman. "Here it is," she said.

The blonde officer looked at the mirror, then handed it back saying, "Okay, you can go. I didn't realize you were a cop."

A blonde decides to try horseback riding, even though she had no prior lessons or experience.

She mounted the horse, unassisted, and the horse immediately sprang into action. It gallops along at a steady and rhythmic pace. However, the blonde begins to slip from the saddle. In terror, she grabs for the horse's mane, but cannot get a firm grip. She tries to throw her arms around the horse's neck but slides down the side of the horse anyway.

The horse gallops along, seemingly impervious to its slipping rider. Finally, giving up her frail grip, the blonde attempts to leap away from the horse, throw herself to safety. Unfortunately, her foot became entangled in the stirrup. She is now at the mercy of the horse's pounding hooves as her head repeatedly strikes the ground.

As her head is being battered, Frank, the Walmart greeter sees her plight and unplugs the horse.

_____

A young blonde woman had all the windows in her house replaced with new double pane, insulated, energy efficient windows. Twelve months later she gets an irate call from the contractor complaining that the work has been done for a year, and despite repeated bills and collection notices, she has yet to make the first payment.

The blonde replies, "Now, don't try to pull a fast one on me. The salesman who sold me the windows told me that in one year they would pay for themselves."

_____

The blonde woman was in the doctor's office. She fell the previous day and believed she may have broken her arm. After the examination, the doctor left the room and returned about 20 minutes later. The blonde asked, "What's taking so long?"

The doctor replied, "I'm just waiting for your x-ray (ex-Ray)."

The blonde says, "I've never dated anyone named Ray." The doctor, "And I think we should do a brain scan."

_____

Two women were at a bar having adult beverages and generally complaining about life. One, a blonde, tells the other, a brunette, and says, "My therapist told me to write letters to people I hate and burn them. I did that. But now I don't know what to do with the letters."

_____

Chapter 4
Crime/Criminals/Police Jokes

One-Liners, Riddles, and Puns

When the police arrest a mime, do they tell him he has the right to remain silent?

_____

Did you hear about the short fortune teller who escaped from prison? She was a small medium at large.

_____

What happened when the Mafia Don crashed his car through a barrier at a construction site and landed in a huge vat of concrete? It turned him into a hardened criminal.

_____

If attacked by a mob of clowns, go for the juggler.

_____

I need everyone to wish me luck. I have a meeting at the bank and if all goes well, I will be out of debt. I'm so excited I can barely put on my ski mask.

_____

What goes, "clop, clop, clop, bang, bang, bang, bang, clop, clop, clop, clop?" An Amish drive-by shooting.

_____

Did you hear about the two guys that stole a calendar? They each got six months.

_____

Who is the strongest man in the world? A bank robber, he holds up banks.

_____

A picture was sitting on the bed in his jail cell, his first day of a long sentence. His cellmate asks, "So, what are you in for?" The picture shouts, "I didn't do anything. I was framed."

_____

Why was the belt arrested? Because it held up some pants.

_____

Stories

Bob is driving down a state highway and sees a hitchhiker at the side of the road. He pulls over and picks up the hitchhiker. The hitchhiker gets in and they take off. The hitchhiker is grateful for the ride and a bit amazed. "I'm surprised in this paranoid climate you would pick me up. How do you know I'm not a weirdo like a serial killer?"

Bob looks at the hitchhiker with a sly grin on his face and says, "I figured the chance is astronomical of two serial killers being in one car."

A guy invites a new female friend over for a drink. While he's making the drinks and snacks, she wanders around the house. They meet in the living room and she asks, "What's your body count?"

The guy stammers, "For, for what?"

The girl replies, "People you've slept with?"

The guy, relieved, says, "Oh! I thought you saw the basement."

The girl, "What?"

The guy, "What? What?"

Bob was a salesman and grew tired of his job. He quit and became a police officer. Several months later, his friend, Dave, asked how he liked his new job. "Well," Bob replied, "the pay is good, and the hours aren't bad. But what I like the best is that the customer is always wrong."

In Municipal Court a woman was found guilty of a traffic violation and was waiting for the judge to render a sentence. The judge asked her occupation. The woman replied, "I'm a schoolteacher."

The judge, a huge smile on his face, said, "Mam, I've waited years for a schoolteacher to appear in this court. Now sit down at that table and write 'I will not run a red light' 100 times."

The two men were opposing each other in court over a relatively minor matter. The judge looks at them and asks, "Why couldn't you guys settle this case out of court?"

"We tried to," one of the men replied. "But the police came and broke it up."

———————

I heard some noise in my garage last night. I thought it was just the cats messing around. So, this morning I'm in the garage and noticed someone stole the limbo stick. Seriously, how low can you go?

———————

The police were investigating the burglary of the house owned by an abstract artist. "So, you got a good look at the guy as he was leaving?" asked one officer.

"That's right," the artist said.

"Can you describe him?"

"I'll do better than that," the abstract artist replied. "I'll draw you a picture of him."

Using the artist's drawing, the police soon arrested a fire hydrant and a stop sign.

———————

A young guy named Chuck bought a horse from a farmer for $250. The farmer agreed to deliver the horse the next day. The next day came and the farmer drove to Chuck's house and said, "Sorry son, but I have some bad news. The horse died."

Chuck replied, "Okay, just give me back my money."

The farmer said, "Well, I can't do that. I already spent the money."

"Then, just bring me the dead horse."

The farmer, curious, asked, "What ya going to do with him?"

"I'm going to raffle him off."

"You can't raffle off a dead horse."

Chuck said, "Sure I can. Watch me. I just won't tell anyone he's dead."

A month later the farmer ran into Chuck and asked, "What happened with the dead horse?"

"I raffled him off. I sold 500 tickets at $5 apiece and made a profit of $2,495."

The farmer said, "Didn't anyone complain?"

Chuck said, "Just the guy who won. So, I gave him back his $5."

It looked bad for Mafia boss Joe Bonnano. The prosecution had several witnesses to the shooting and the murder weapon had Bonanno's fingerprints on it.

"Don't worry," his lawyer said. "I've bribed one of the jurors. I'll cost you 20 grand, but he's going to hold out for a manslaughter conviction."

The case ended and the jury began deliberation. They were out for three days, but finally returned with a manslaughter conviction. Bonanno got five years and his lawyer told him how lucky he was to get off so lightly.

That evening the lawyer met the bribed juror. "You had me worried," the lawyer said. "Why did it take so long to reach a decision?"

"It wasn't easy," the juror said. "The other 11 people wanted to acquit him, but I argued them out of it."

Boy, what a strange day. I'm walking down the street and find this hat full of money—lucky me. Then suddenly, this angry guy with a guitar is chasing me.

Late one night a burglar breaks into a house. While he was sneaking around looking for things to steal, a creepy voice says, "Jesus is watching you." The burglar looks around, sees nothing and keeps moving. Again, he hears the strange voice, "Jesus is watching you." In a dark corner he sees a cage containing a bird. He walks over and asks the bird, a parrot, "Was it you who said Jesus was watching me?"

The parrot replied, "Yes."

Relieved, the burglar asked the parrot its name.

"Clarence," the parrot answered.

"That's a pretty dumb name for a parrot. What idiot named you Clarence?" the burglar inquired.

The parrot answered, "The same idiot who named the Rottweiler Jesus."

Chapter 5
Doctor/Medical Jokes

One-Liners, Riddles, and Puns

Did you hear that a huge truck carrying a zillion cases of Vicks Vapor Rub overturned on Interstate 15? Amazingly, there was no congestion for eight hours.

Birthdays are good for your health. Many studies show that people who have more birthdays live longer.

I'm on the Dr. Atkinson diet. Harvey Atkinson is a dentist in Cedar City whose philosophy is, "Eat what tastes good and clean your plate."

Why are hallways in psychiatric hospitals called "hallways?" Shouldn't they be called psycho paths (psychopaths)?

When is a doctor most annoyed? When he is out of patients (patience).

A man wakes up in the hospital after a serious accident. He shouts, "Doctor, doctor, I can't feel my legs.!"

The doctor calmly replies, "I know you can't, I've cut off your arms."

What did one tonsil say to the other? "Get dressed, the doctor's taking us out tonight."

Stories

During a visit to the local mental asylum, Bob asked the director, "How do you determine whether or not a patient should be institutionalized?"

"Well," the director said, "we fill up a bathtub with water then offer a teaspoon, a teacup, and a bucket to the patient and ask him or her to empty the bathtub."

"Oh, I understand," said Bob. "a normal person would use the bucket because its bigger than a spoon or teacup."

"No," the director replied. "A normal person would just pull the plug. Do you want a bed near the window?"

After a lengthy examination, a doctor walks into the examination room and puts his hand on the patient's shoulder. "I'm afraid I have some bad news. You're dying and you don't have much time left."

"No!" the patient shouted. "How much time do I have?"

"Ten," the doctor said.

"Ten what?" cried the patient. "Years, months, days?"

The doctor calmly replies, "Nine, eight ...."

Two Kentucky hillbillies, Jimmy Bob and Billy Bob, walk into a diner. They both order the daily special, fried squirrel. While having a bite to eat, they talk about their moonshine operation. Suddenly, a woman at a nearby table eating a fried possum sandwich begins to cough.

After a minute or so, it becomes apparent that she is in real distress. Jimmy Bob looks at her and says, "Kin ya swallar?" The woman shakes her head no. Then he asks, "Kin ya breathe?" The woman begins to turn blue, and shakes her head no.

Then Jimmy Bob walks over to the woman, lifts her dress, yanks down her drawers, and quickly gives her right butt cheek a lick with his tongue.

The woman is so shocked that she has a violent spasm, and a big chunk of fried possum sandwich flies out of her mouth.

She begins to breathe again and, after righting her clothes, profusely thanks Jimmy Bob.

The Hillbilly walks slowly back to his table. Jimmy Bob says to Billy Bob, "Ya know, I saved that lady's life. I read about this way to help people who are choking, but I never seen anyone do it. It's called the Hind Lick (Heimlich) Maneuver."

Shortly before his scheduled operation, a man in a wheelchair was wheeling himself frantically down a hospital hallway. A nurse stopped him and asked, "Whoa, what's the matter?"

The guy said, "I heard another nurse say 'It's a very simple operation, don't worry. I'm sure it will be fine.'"

"She was just trying to comfort you. What's so frightening about that?" the nurse said.

The guy nearly yelled, "She wasn't talking to me. She was talking to the doctor."

Henry is getting a physical at the doctor's office. A nurse has taken his blood pressure, height, and weight. She sticks a thermometer in his mouth and then exits the room. Henry hears her ask another nurse in the hall, "Remind me again how you tell the regular thermometers from the rectal ones?"

A patient was lying in bed, still groggy from the effects of his recent operation. His doctor comes in looking very glum.

"I can't be sure what's wrong with you," the doctor tells him. "I think it's the drinking."

"Okay," the patient said. "Can we get an opinion from a doctor who's sober?"

A kid broke her arm and was in the doctor's office getting a cast. She asked, "Doctor, how long will my arm be in a cast?"

"At least six weeks."

"When you remove it, will I be able to play the violin?"

"Of course," the doctor replied.

Wow," the kid said. "That's great. I could never play it before."

Examining the x-rays and test results, the doctor said, "Not a thing to worry about. You should live to be 90."

"But, doctor," the patient said, "I am 90."

"See, I was right," the doctor replied.

"That tooth is badly infected and has to come out," a dentist told his patient.

"How much will it cost?" the patient asked.

"Two hundred dollars," the dentist answered.

Sitting upright, the patient blurted, "What? Two hundred dollars? For a couple of minutes work? That's robbery."

"Well," the dentist calmly replied, "if it makes you feel any better, I can extract the tooth very, veerry slowly."

John just completed his annual physical. The doctor studied the results and said, "The best thing for you is to cut out all sweets, give up alcohol, and stop smoking."

"I see," John said. "To be honest, I don't deserve the best. What's the second best?"

Barbie had been seeing the psychiatrist for years, pouring out her heart and soul to him once a week. However, she wasn't making any progress, and the doctor didn't believe she ever would.

"Barbie," he said at the end of one session, "do you think these visits are doing you any good?"

"Not really," she said. "My inferiority complex is as strong as ever."

"Barbie," the psychiatrist remarked, "I have something to tell you. You don't have an inferiority complex. You are, in fact, inferior."

Chapter 6
Don't Fit in Any Other Category Jokes

One-Liners, Riddles, and Puns

It's a shame nothing is built in the USA any longer. I just bought a TV and the label said, "Built in antenna." Hell, I don't even know where that is.

If the zombie apocalypse ever happens, go to Costco. The building is massive with concrete walls, contains years of food and supplies, and best of all the zombies can't get in without a Costco membership card.

Here's a question, do you know where Engagement, Ohio is located? Don't know? It is between Dayton (dating) and Marion (marryin'), Ohio.

I was at an emotional wedding last week. Even the cake was in tiers (tears).

Why don't cannibals eat clowns? Because they taste funny.

I did a theatrical performance about puns. It was a play on words.

This guy is crossing the border into Canada and the border guard asked if he had any firearms. The guy says, "Sure, what do you need?"

A day without sunshine is like … night.

How do crazy people go through a forest? They take the psychopath.

The other day I held the door open for a clown. It was a nice gesture (jester).

No matter how much you push the envelope, it'll still be stationary.

I put my grandma on speed dial. I call that Instagram.

Never argue with stupid people. They will drag you down to their level and beat you with experience.
Mark Twain

What do you call a boomerang that doesn't work? A stick.

How are a Texas tornado and a Tennessee divorce similar? In both of them somebody's gonna lose a trailer.

Something to think about: Do peasants ever actually wear peasant blouses?

Why was the skeleton afraid to cross the road? Because he didn't have any guts.

Two antennas met on a roof, fell in love, and got married. The ceremony wasn't much but the reception was excellent.

The invisible man married the invisible woman. Their kids were nothing to look at either.

Who was the roundest knight at King Arthur's round table? Sir Cumference (circumference). He gained his size by eating too much pie (pi).

Did you know that a grenade thrown in a kitchen in France results in Linoleum Blownapart (Napoleon Bonaparte)?

Two hats were hanging on a hat rack. One says to the other, "You stay here, I'll go on a head."

I hate it when TV shows flash a warning that the forth coming show contains "adult material" and then don't show anyone going to work, paying bills, cleaning the house, or trying to get the kids out of bed.

What is round on both ends and "hi" in the middle? Ohio.

_____

No one ever told us how much of our adult life we'd spend pretending to look at random items is a food store aisle while waiting for someone to move his/her shopping cart out of the way.

_____

If you ever fall over in public, pick yourself up and say, "sorry, it's been a while since I inhabited a living body." And just walk away.

_____

Bob bought a pair of shoes from a drug dealer. He didn't know what he laced them with, but he's been tripping all day.

_____

Which letter in the word "scent" is silent? The "s" or the "c"?

_____

Is there a fourth of July in England? Yes, it comes after the third of July.

_____

How many birthdays does the average American have? One, all the rest are anniversaries of the birth day.

_____

Some months have 31 days. How many have 28 days? All of them.

_____

Is it legal in Utah for a man to marry his widow's sister? No, because he is dead.

_____

A pun has not completely matured until it is full grown (groan).

_____

A guy went to a bookstore and asks the clerk, "Where's the self-help section?" The clerk replies, "If I told you, that would defeat the purpose."

_____

There are three types of people, those who can count and those who can't.

_____

Where did Captain Hook buy his hook? At the second-hand store.

_____

Tradition is just peer pressure from dead people.

_____

Why did the soldier salute the refrigerator? Because it was General Electric.

_____

What kind of house weighs the least? A lighthouse.

_____

What did the beach say as the tide came in? Long time, no sea (see).

_____

What did one elevator say to the other? I think I'm coming down with something.

_____

What has a face, but cannot see? A clock

_____

What goes up yet never comes down? Your age.

_____

What's the difference between a kleptomaniac and a literalist? The literalist takes things literally. The kleptomaniac takes things, literally.

_____

What is bought by the yard and worn by the foot? Carpet.

_____

When is a door not a door? When it's ajar (a jar).

_____

What was the highest mountain before Mt. Everest was discovered? Mt. Everest.

_____

What word does everyone pronounce wrong? "Wrong".

_____

Why was the math book sad? Because it had too many problems.

_____

How many books can you put in an empty bag? One. After that, it is not empty.

_____

Where does a tree store their stuff? In its trunk.

_____

Why did the tree go to the dentist? Because it needed a root canal.

_____

What kind of tree can fit in your hand? A palm tree.

_____

Why is an old car like a baby's toy? They both rattle.

_____

What did one wall say to the other? I'll meet you at the corner.

_____

How were the first European Americans similar to ants? They both lived in colonies.

_____

What do Alexander the Great and Kermit the Frog have in common? The same middle name, "the."

_____

When can three very large people get under one umbrella and not get wet? When it's not raining.

_____

Stories

John, photographer for a local newspaper, was told a twin-engine plane would be waiting for him at the airport.

Arriving, he spotted a twin-engine plane warming up outside the hanger. He jumped in and said, "Let's go."

The pilot taxied and took off.

Once in the air, John told the pilot, "Fly low over the valley so I take photos of the fire spreading in the hills."

The pilot, "Why?

John replied, "Because I'm a photographer for the local newspaper and I need to get some close-up shots of the fire."

The pilot was strangely silent for a moment, then stammered, "So, what you're telling me is … You're not my flying instructor?"

A group of chess enthusiasts checked into a hotel and were standing in the lobby discussing their latest tournament victories. After about an hour, the manager came out of his office and asked them to disperse.

"But why," they asked as they moved off.

"Because," the manager replied, "I can't stand chess-nuts boasting in an open foyer." (chestnuts roasting on an open fire)

A truck loaded with thousands of copies of *Roget's Thesaurus* crashed yesterday losing its entire load. Witnesses were stunned, startled, aghast, taken aback, stupefied, confused, shocked, rattled, paralyses, dazed, bewildered, mixed up, surprised, awed, dumbfounded, nonplussed, flabbergasted, astounded, amazed, confounded, astonished, overwhelmed, horrified, numbed, speechless, and perplexed.

Bob concluded he needed to explore the full dimensions of existence and decided to go to a psychic. He Googled "psychics" and found a Madam Rosinka nearby who works out of her house. He walks to her place and knocks on the front door. He hears a woman yelling from inside, "Who is it?"

Bob left.

A woman gives birth to identical twins and gives them up for adoption. One goes to a family in Egypt and is named "Amal." The other goes to a family in Spain; they name him "Juan." Years later, Juan sends a picture of himself to his birth mother. Upon receiving the photo, she tells her husband that she wishes she had a photo of Amal. Her husband responds, "They're identical twins. If you've seen Juan (one), you've seen Amal ('em all)."

Johnny opened the morning newspaper and was dumbfounded to read his own obituary. What? He didn't recall dying. He quickly phoned his best friend, Dave. "Did you read the morning newspaper?" asked Johnny. "It contains my obituary. They say I died."

"Yes, I saw it," replied Dave. "Where are you calling from?"

A farmer stood leaning on a fence at the edge of his property surveying his domain. He watched as a red sports car crested a hill, roared down the road, and came to a screeching stop near the farmer.

The driver looked at the farmer and asked, "Do you know how I can get to Interstate 15?"

The farmer thought for a few seconds and then said, "Nope."

"Do you know where the nearest freeway onramp is?" the driver asked.

"Nope."

"How about the town of Santa Clara? Do you know which direction it is from here?"

"Nope."

Frustrated, the driver raced his engine and said, "you don't know much, do you?"

"Nope," the farmer replied. "But I'm not lost."

Bob was on his way to the cemetery to see the grave of an old friend who died suddenly, and he had not seen in many years. He was not familiar with the cemetery and programmed his GPS to provide directions. He felt a bit uncomfortable turning into the cemetery and the GPS said, "You have reached your final destination."

Chapter 7
Ethnic Jokes

One-Liners, Riddles, and Puns

Did you hear about the $3,000,000 Polish lottery? The winner gets $3 a year for a million years.

_____

What do you call a member of the Irish Republican Army who carries a snub nose .38 and a switchblade? A pacifist.

_____

If the Japanese are such technological giants, why do they still eat with sticks?

_____

What do you call an Arab Elvis impersonator? Amal Shookup (I'm all shook up).

_____

What's Irish and sits around the pool? Paddy O'Furniture (patio furniture).

_____

The word "karaoke" comes from an old Japanese saying meaning, "Go home, you're drunk."

_____

I just heard on the radio that the French are expecting a terrorist attack. Something bad is going on. The government has raised the terror alert status from run to hide. The only two higher levels are surrender and collaborate.

_____

In Western countries, parents feed their babies with tiny spoons and forks. So, in countries where most people eat with chopsticks do parents feed their babies with toothpicks?

_____

What do you call a fake stone in Ireland? A sham rock (shamrock).

_____

Stories

One day an Irishman who had been stranded on a deserted island for 10 years saw a speck on the horizon. He thought to himself, "It's certainly not a ship."

As the speck got closer, he ruled out the possibilities of a small boat or raft. Suddenly a figure clad in a wet suit appeared and strode up the beach.

Putting aside the scuba tanks and mask and zipping down the top of the wet suit stood a drop dead gorgeous blonde woman. She walked up to the stunned Irishman and said, "Tell me, how long has it been since you had a good cigarette?"

"Ten years," replied the amazed Irishman.

With that, she unzipped a waterproof pocket on the left sleeve of the wet suit and pull out a fresh pack of cigarettes and a lighter. He removed a cigarette from the pack, lit it, and took a long drag. "Faith and begorrah," said the castaway. I'd almost forgotten how great a smoke can be."

"And how long has it been since you had a drop of good Jameson's Irish Whiskey?" asked the blonde.

The Irishman replied, "Ten years." Hearing that the blonde reached over to her right sleeve, unzipped a pocket there, removed a flask, and handed it to him. He opened the flask and took a long drink. "Tis nectar of the gods!" shouted the Irishman.

At this point the blonde started slowly unzipping the front of her wet suit. She looked at the trembling man and asked, "And how long has it been since you played around (a round)?" The Irishman was stunned, "Jesus, Mary, and Joseph! Don't tell me you've got golf clubs in there too!"

Two men were sitting next to each other at O'Malley's Pub in London. After a while, one bloke looks at the other and says, "I can't help but think, from listening to you, that you're from Ireland."

The second bloke responds proudly, "Yes, that I am."

The first one says, "So am I. And where about in Ireland might you be from?"

The second guy answers, "I'm from Dublin, I am."

The first guy responds, "And so am I."

"Mother Mary and begore. And what street did you live on in Dublin?" asks the second guy.

"A lovely little area it was. I lived on McCleary Street in the old central part of town," replied the first guy.

Amazed, the second Irishman says, "So did I. And what school did you attend?"

The first Irishman answers, "Well now, I went to St. Mary's."

The second guy gets really excited and says, "So did I. What year did you graduate?"

"I graduated in 1964," says the first guy.

The second Irishman exclaims, "The good lord must be smiling down on us! I can hardly believe our good luck at winding up in the same place tonight. Can you believe it, I graduated from St. Mary's in 1964 my own self."

About this time, Vicky walks up to the bar, sits down, and orders a drink.

Brian, the bartender, walks over to Vicky, shakes his head and mutters, "It's going to be a long night tonight."

Vicky asks, "Why do you say that Brian?"

He replies, "The Murphy twins are drunk again."

_____

Chapter 8
Food/Diet/Eating Jokes

One-Liners, Riddles, and Puns

Did you know the first French fry was not cooked in France? Where was it cooked then? In grease (Greece).

Carrots may be good for your eyes, but booze will double your vision.

Vegetarian is an old Indian word for "crappy hunter."

Did you hear about the guy who got a job at a bakery because he kneaded (needed) dough?

Do vegetarians eat animal cookies?

After a good dinner, one can forgive anything, even one's own relatives. Oscar Wilde

---

What did Mr. and Mrs. Hamburger name their new daughter? Patty, of course.

Did you hear about the new restaurant that just opened on the moon? Good food, but no atmosphere.

What do you call cheese that isn't yours? Nacho (not yo) cheese.

Life expectancy would grow by leaps and bounds if green vegetables smelled as good as bacon.

I just stepped on a corn flake. Uh oh, now I'm officially a cereal (serial) killer.

Don't tell secrets in the garden. The potatoes have eyes, the corn has ears, and the beanstalk (beans talk).

_____

I want to lose weight, but I don't want to get caught up in one of those "eat right and exercise" scams.

_____

What kind of pastry come with a thesaurus? Synonym (cinnamon) rolls.

_____

Two women were sitting in a bar lamenting their weight and their current diets. One says, "My fitness goal is to get down to what I told the DMV I weigh."

_____

Why did the jelly roll? Because it saw the apple turn over.

_____

What is a pickle's favorite game show? Let's Make a Dill (Deal).

_____

What did one potato chip say to the other? Let's go for a dip.

_____

What has ears but cannot hear? Corn.

_____

What did cured ham actually have?

_____

Why are chefs cruel? Because they beat eggs and whip cream.

_____

What do you get if you cross a sweet potato and a jazz musician? A yam (jam) session.

_____

When do you go at red and stop at green? When eating a watermelon.

_____

What do you use to repair a tomato? Tomato paste.

_____

What did one plate say to the other? Dinner's on me.

_____

Why do the French like to eat snails? Because they don't like fast food.

_____

Why shouldn't you tell a joke to an egg? Because it might crack up.

_____

What do you give a sick lemon? Lemon aid (lemonade).

_____

Stories

A tomato family, the Romas, is walking down the road. The kid tomato is messing around and not keeping up. The dad tomato yells at him, which works for a while. But soon the kid is way behind. The dad tomato goes back to the kid and smacks him on the head and says, "catch up" (ketchup).

_____

A woman went to a local fast food joint and ordered a taco. She told the employee she wanted "minimal lettuce" on the taco.

The fast food employee replied that he was sorry, but they only had iceberg lettuce.

_____

Two women were sitting in a bar lamenting their weight and their current diets. One says, "I've decided I'll never get down to my original weight, and I'm okay with that. After all, 6 pounds 3 ounces is just not realistic."

_____

Bob was dining at a fancy restaurant. His food arrived, he stared at the plate, and told the waiter, "I don't like the looks of this codfish."

"Sir, if you're interested in looks, you should have ordered goldfish," the waiter replied.

_____

Jane and Cathy went to a diner that looked like it had seen better days. As they slid into a booth, Jane wiped some crumbs from the seat. Then she took a napkin and wiped some spilled liquid from the tabletop. The waitress came and asked if they wanted menus.

"No thanks," Cathy said. "I'll just have a cup of regular coffee."

"I'll have a cup of coffee, too," Jane said. "And please make sure the cup is clean."

The waitress shot Jane a dirty look, then turned and walked into the kitchen. Two minutes later, she was back.

"Two cups of regular coffee," she announced. "Which one of you wanted the clean cup?"

A couple of guys were having a few drinks at the local bar. One turns to the other and says, "I read an article today that said humans eat more bananas than monkeys." The second guy, "Well, sure. I can't remember the last time I ate a monkey."

Chapter 9
Gross Jokes

One-Liners, Riddles, and Puns

Jeffrey Dahmer has his mother over for dinner. While eating, she says, "Jeffrey, I don't like your friends."

Jeffrey replies, "Well mom, then just eat the vegetables."

A friend will help you move. A really good friend will help you move a body.

Stories

Two women are sitting in a bar and strike up a conversation. After chatting awhile, they begin exchanging gripes. The first woman says, "My husband is a hunter and he wants me to learn how to skin and cook his kills." The second woman says, "That doesn't sound too bad." The first woman replies, "He's a serial killer."

My full-tine job is being a clown for kids' parties. Mostly it is fun. However, explaining to a child that we're mortal and that death is inescapable is by far the hardest part of being a party clown.

Chapter 10
Lawyer Jokes

One-Liners, Riddles, and Puns

Two men met on the street. The first one says, "It was really cold this morning."

"How cold was it?" asked the second.

The first guy replied, "I don't know the exact temperature, but I saw a lawyer with his hands in his own pockets."

What's the difference between a lawyer and a catfish? One's a bottom dwelling scum sucker and the other is a fish.

What do you call skydiving lawyers? Skeet.

What's the difference between a dead skunk on the road and a dead lawyer on the road? The dead skunk has skid marks before it.

Stories

One day the gate between heaven and hell breaks down. St. Peter arrives on the scene and calls out for the devil. The devil saunters over and says, "What do you want?"

St. Peter says, "As per our agreement, it's your turn to fix the gate."

The devil replies, "I'm sorry but my work crew is too busy to worry about fixing a mere gate."

"Well then," says St. Peter, "I'll have to sue you for breaking our agreement."

The devil smirks and says, "Oh yeah? Where are you going to get a lawyer?"
Soupy Sales

A rabbi, a Hindu, and a lawyer were driving together late one night in the country when their car expired. They set out to find help and came to a farmhouse. When they knocked upon the door, the farmer explained that he had only two beds and one of the men would have to sleep in the barn with the animals.

The rabbi said he would sleep in the barn and let the other two have the beds. Ten minutes after the rabbi left, there was a knock on the bedroom door. The rabbi entered exclaiming, "I can't sleep in the barn, there's a pig in there. It's against my religion to sleep in the same room with a pig."

The Hindu said he would sleep in the barn, since he had no religious problems with pigs. However, about five minutes later the Hindu burst through the bedroom door saying, "There's a cow in the barn! I can't sleep in the same room as a cow. It's against my religion."

The lawyer, anxious to get to sleep, said he would go to the barn since he had no problem sleeping in the same room as animals. Two minutes later the bedroom door burst open and the pig and cow entered ...

A very successful attorney parked his new Lexus in front of his office, ready to show it off to his colleagues.

As he was getting out, a truck came along too close, completely tore off the driver's door, and stopped down the road.

Fortunately, a cop in a police car was close enough to see the accident and pulled up behind the Lexus.

Before the cop had a chance to ask any questions the attorney started screaming hysterically about how his Lexus, which he had purchased the day before, was completely ruined and would never be the same no matter how any auto body shop tried to make it new again.

After the lawyer finally wound down, the cop shook his head in disbelief. "I can't believe how materialistic you lawyers are," he said. "You are so focused on your possessions that you ignore the most important things in life."

"How can you say such a thing?" asked the lawyer.

The cop replied, "don't you even realize that your left arm is missing? It was severed when the truck hit you."

"Oh my god!" screamed the lawyer. "My Rolex."

Recently a teacher, a garbage collector, and a lawyer all died and wound up together at the Pearly Gates. St. Peter informed them that in order to get into Heaven, they would have to correctly answer one question.

St. Peter addressed the teacher, "What was the name of the large passenger ship that crashed into an iceberg? A movie was made about the tragedy."

The teacher answered quickly, "The Titanic." St. Peter let him through the gate.

St. Peter turned to the garbage collector. Heaven didn't need the garbage odor, so St. Peter asked a somewhat more difficult question, "How many people died when the Titanic sank?"

Fortunately, the trash guy had recently seen the movie on TV and answered, "1,228." That's right, you may enter," said St. Peter.

St. Peter turned to the lawyer, "Name the 1,228 Titanic victims."

———————

A blonde finds herself sitting next to a lawyer on an airplane.

The lawyer keeps bugging the blonde wanting her to play a game of intelligence.

Finally, the lawyer offers her 10 to 1 odds, and says every time the blonde cannot answer one of his questions, she owes him $5, but every time he cannot answer hers, he'll give her $50. The lawyer figures he cannot lose, after all he was playing against a blonde.

The lawyer begins by asking, "What is the distance between the sun and the earth?"

Without saying a word, the blonde digs into her purse and hands him $5. She then asks, "What goes up a hill with three legs and comes back down the hill with four legs?"

The lawyer is puzzled. He looks up the question on his laptop, calls friends trying to find the answer. After a couple of hours, angry and frustrated, he gives up and gives the blonde $50.

He wants the answer and asks the blonde "What is the answer to your question?"

Without saying anything the blonde hands him $5.

———————

Chapter 11
Men/Women/Relationship Jokes

One-Liners, Riddles, and Puns

A wife was going through her wardrobe and said, "Look at this, it still fits me after 25 years."

Her husband replied, "It's a scarf." His body is yet to be found.

Arguing with a woman is like reading the software license agreement. In the end, you ignore everything and click "I agree."

At a wedding party recently someone yelled, "All married people please stand next to the one person who has made your life worth living." The bartender was almost crushed to death.

My wife says I have only two faults. I don't listen and some other shit she was rattling on about.

Whenever I'm with my family and someone says, "Wow, you have a beautiful family!" I reply, "Well, we left the ugly ones at home."

The other day my wife just stopped and said, "You weren't even listening to a word I said."

I thought, "That's a pretty weird way to start a conversation."

For those who do not want Alexa listening to their conversations, Amazon is making a male version called Alex . . . it doesn't listen to anything.

One woman was overheard telling another woman, "My husband gets so mad when I introduce him as my first husband."

You know those adorable idiosyncrasies you loved when first dating? After 20 years of marriage they become what police refer to as "motive."

———————

How can you tell if your husband has died? His conversation skills are about the same, but he no longer hogs the remote.

———————

How are men and government bonds similar? They both take a long time to mature.

———————

How are men different from government bonds? Government bonds eventually mature.

———————

She was only a whiskey maker, but he loved her still.

———————

Go for younger men. You might as well ... they never mature anyway.

———————

Men are all the same. They just have different faces so you can tell them apart.

———————

Definition of a bachelor: A man who has missed the opportunity to make some woman miserable.

———————

Women don't make fools of men. Most of them are the do-it-yourself types.

———————

If he asks what sort of books you're interested in, tell him checkbooks.

———————

Men to women: Come to us with a problem only if you want help solving it. That's what we do. Sympathy is what your girlfriends are for.

———————

Men to women: Anything we said six months ago is inadmissible in an argument. In fact, all comments are null and void after seven days.

———————

Men to women: If you think you're fat, you probably are. Don't ask us.

_____

Men to women: If something we said can be interpreted in two ways and one of the ways makes you sad or angry, we meant the other one.

_____

Men to women: You can either ask us to do something or tell us how you want it done. Not both. If you already know best how to do it, just do it yourself.

_____

Men to women: Whenever possible, please say whatever you have to say during the commercials.

_____

Women who say getting married was the best day of their lives have obviously never had two KitKats fall out a vending machine by mistake.

_____

What is the difference between men and pigs? Pigs don't turn into men when they drink.

_____

Why's beauty more important than brains for a woman? Because plenty of men are stupid, but not very many are blind.

_____

I'm so single right now that if I stood on a cliff and shouted, "I love you," my echo would say, "I just want to be friends."

_____

Did you hear about the new "Divorce Barbie?" She comes with all of Ken's stuff.

_____

Men to women: All men see in only 16 colors. The Windows default setting for peach, for example, is a fruit, not a color. Pumpkin is also a fruit. We have no idea what mauve is.

_____

Men to women: If we ask what is wrong and you say "nothing," we will act like nothing's wrong. We know you are lying, but it is not worth the hassle.

A wife says to her husband, "Of course, I remember when we got married. What I can't remember is why."

Things my mother taught me:

My mother taught me to appreciate a job well done. "If you're going to kill each other, do it outside. I just finished cleaning."

My mother taught me religion: "You better pray that will come out of the carpet."

My mother taught me about time travel: "If you don't straighten up, I'm going to knock you into the middle of next week."

My mother taught me logic: "Because I said so, that's why."

My mother taught me foresight: "Make sure you wear clean underwear, in case you're in an accident."

My mother taught me irony: "Keep crying and I'll give you something to cry about."

My mother taught me about contortionism: "Will you look at that dirt on the back of your neck."

My mother taught me about stamina: "You'll sit there until all that broccoli is gone."

Stories

What is celibacy? Celibacy can be a choice in life, or a condition imposed by circumstances.

While attending a "Make Your Marriage Better" weekend seminar, Frank and his wife Ann listened to the instructor declare, "It is essential that husbands and wives know the things that are important to each other."

The instructor then addressed the men. "Can you name and describe your wife's favorite flower?"

Frank leaned over, touched Ann's arm, and whispered, "Gold Medal-All-Purpose, isn't it?"

65

And thus began Frank's life of celibacy.

A father buys a lie detector robot that slaps people when they tell a lie. He decides to test it at dinner one night. The father asks his son what he did that afternoon.

The son said, "I did some schoolwork." The robot slaps the son. The son says, "Okay, okay. I was at a friend's house watching movies."

Dad asks, "What kind of movies did you watch?"

Son replies, *Toy Story.* The robot smacks the son. "Okay, okay, we were watching porn."

Dad says, "What? At your age I didn't even know what porn was."

The robot slaps the father. Mom laughs and says, "Well, he certainly is your son." The robot slaps the mother.

A young boy asks his dad, "Is it true dad, that in some parts of Africa a man doesn't know his wife until her marries her?"

Dad replies, "Son, that happens in every country."

A couple of women were having a drink at a posh restaurant. The first one says, "So what do you think happiness is?"

The second one replied, "I never knew what real happiness was until I got married, and by then it was too late."

Bob was at the doctors and said, "I'm not able to do all the things around the house that I used to do."

The doctor gave him a complete examination and said, "Well, in plain English, you're just a lazy bum."

"Thank you," Bob said. "Now please give me the medical term for lazy bum that I can tell my wife."

The bride came down the aisle and when she reached the alter, the groom was standing there with his golf bag filled with clubs.

She says, "What are your gold clubs doing here?"

The groom looks her in the eye and says, "This isn't going to take all day, is it?"

_____

A married couple had been out shopping at the mall for most of the afternoon, suddenly, the wife realized that her husband had "disappeared."

The somewhat irate spouse called her mate's cell phone and demanded, "Where the hell are you?"

The husband replied, "Darling you remember that jewelry shop where you saw the diamond necklace and totally fell in love with it and I didn't have money that time and said baby it'll be yours one day."

The wife, with a smile blushing said, "Yes, I remember that my love."

Husband, "Well, I'm in the bar next to that shop."

_____

An old guy is riding his motorcycle along California Highway 1, the road that hugs the coast. He stops to admire the view and suddenly the booming voice of God comes from the sky, "Because you have been a good guy for all your years, I'll grant you one wish."

The biker thinks about this and says, "I've always wanted to go to Hawaii, but couldn't afford it. Can you build a bridge to Hawaii so I can ride my bike there?"

The voice says, "That is a pretty materialistic wish. Think of the enormous challenge it would pose: the bridge supports reaching the bottom of the Pacific Ocean, the concrete and steel it would take, and so on. It would nearly exhaust natural resources. Take a minute and think of something that might help humanity."

The biker thinks about it and says, "How about this, I wish all men could understand women. How they feel, what they are thinking. Why when you take your wife to a nice anniversary dinner at Arby's they aren't pleased. How can I/all men truly make a woman happy."

The voice replied, "Do you want two or four lanes on the bridge?"

_____

An elderly couple were killed in an accident and found themselves being given a tour of heaven by St. Peter.

"Here is your oceanside condo, over there are tennis courts, swimming pool, two golf courses. If you need refreshments, just stop by the many restaurants and bars located in the area."

"Heck, Gloria," the old man hissed when St. Peter walked off, "we could have been here ten years ago if you hadn't read all about that stupid oat bran, wheat germ, and low-fat diets."

A husband and wife are sitting on the couch watching TV. The wife turns to the husband and talks to him. What he hears, "Honey, how would you like me to put your head in a bench vise and turn the handle until your skull squished?"

What she said was, "Honey, how would you like to turn off the TV and talk?"

Wife asks her husband, "What are you doing?"

Husband, "Nothing."

Wife, "Nothing? You've been reading our marriage certificate for an hour."

Husband, "I was looking for the expiration date."

A young woman tells her boyfriend, "When we get married, I want to share all your worries, troubles and lighten your burden."

The young man replies, "That's very kind of you, darling, but I don't have any worries or troubles."

The young woman says, "Well, that's because we aren't married yet."

A little boy tells his mom, "Mom, when I was on the bus with dad this morning, he told me to give up my seat for a lady who was standing."

Mom says, "Well, you did the right thing."

Little boy, "But mom, I was sitting on daddy's lap."

A newly married man asks his wife, "Would you have married me even if my father hadn't left me a fortune?"

"Honey," the wife replied sweetly, "I'd have married you no matter who left you a fortune."

———————

A man was sitting on the couch reading a book when his wife smacks him on the head with a frying pan. "What was that for?" the man asked.

The wife replied, "That was for the piece of paper with the name Jenny on it that I found in your pants pocket."

The husband then said, "When I was at the horse races last week, Jenny was the name of one of the horses I bet on."

The wife apologized and started doing housework.

Three days later the man is watching TV when his wife bonks him on the head with a baseball bat, knocking him unconsciousness.

Upon regaining consciousness, the man asked why she had almost killed him.

The wife replied, "Your horse phoned."

———————

Mary goes up to Father O'Grady after his Sunday morning service and she is in tears. Father O'Grady asks, "What's bothering you dear?"

Mary says, "Oh Father, I've got terrible news. My husband passed away last night."

The priest says, "Mary, that's terrible. Tell me, did he have any last requests?"

Mary replies, "That he did Father."

"What did he ask, Mary?"

She says, "He said, 'Please Mary, put down that gun."

———————

A husband and wife were shopping at the supermarket. The husband picks up a case of Budweiser and puts it into the cart. "What do you think you're doing?" asks his wife.

"They're on sale, only $10 for 24 cans," the husband replies.

"Put them back, we can't afford that," demands the wife.

They carry on with their shopping. A few aisles later, the woman picks up a $20 jar of face cream and puts in the cart.

"What do you think you're doing?" asked the husband.

"It's my face cream. It makes me look beautiful," replies the wife.

"So does 24 cans of Budweiser and it's half the price of face cream."

The manager was astounded that a murder took place in his store.

A mom was out walking with her five year old daughter. The daughter picked up something off the ground and started to put it into her mouth.

The mom took the thing away from the little girl and asked her not to do that.

"Why?" the daughter asked.

"Because it's been on the ground, it's dirty, and it probably has germs," the mom said.

At this point, the little girl looked at her mom with absolute admiration and asked, "Mom, how do you know all this stuff? You are so smart."

The mom thought quickly and replied, "All moms know this stuff. It's on the Mom Test. You have to know it, or they won't let you be a mom."

The mom and daughter walked along in silence for a couple of minutes. The daughter was obviously pondering this new information.

"Oh, I get it!" she beamed, "So if you don't pass the test, you have to be the dad."

"Exactly," the mom said.

Jerry went to a bar the other night and overheard three very hefty women talking. Their accent sounded Scottish, so Jerry walked over and asked, "Hello ladies. Are you three lassies from Scotland?"

One of them angrily screeched, "It's Wales, you bloody idiot, Wales!"

Jerry apologized and replied, "I'm so sorry. And are you three whales from Scotland?"

That was the last thing Jerry remembered.

This husband is looking through the newspaper and came upon a story that reported on a study saying women use more words than men. The study stated, "Men use about 15,000 words per day, while women use approximately 30,000."

Excited to prove to his wife that he had been right all along when he claimed she talked too much, he showed her the story. The wife thought for a while, then finally said, "If women use more words, it's because we have to repeat just about everything we say."

The husband said, "What?"

———————

Bob was sitting on the edge of the bed watching his wife, Molly, who was looking at herself in the mirror. Since her birthday was not far off, Bob asked what she'd like as a gift. "I'd like to be eight again,' she replied, still looking in the mirror.

On the morning of her birthday, Bob rose early, made her a nice bowl of Coco Pops, and then took her to Adventure World theme park. What a day! They rode every ride in the park—the Death Slide, the Wall of Fear, the Screaming Roller Coaster, and more.

Five hours later they staggered out of the theme park. Molly's head was reeling, and her stomach felt upside down.

Bob took her to a McDonald's where he bought her a Happy Meal.

Then it was off to a movie with popcorn and soda. What a great adventure.

Finally, they wobbled home and collapsed into bed, exhausted. Bob leaned over Molly with a big smile and asked, "Well dear, what was it like being eight again?"

Molly's eyes opened slowly she snarled, "I meant my dress size, you idiot."

———————

A guy is fed up and wants a divorce. He is in divorce court and tells the judge, "I just can't take it anymore. Every night she's out until way after midnight, just going from bar to bar."

The judge asks, "Why is she doing this? What's she doing?"

The guy answers, "She's looking for me."

———————

A guy goes to the police station to report a stolen credit card. The cop taking the report asked the guy why it took him five months to report the stolen card. The guy replied, "Until recently, the thief was spending less than my wife."

One day the housework-challenged husband decided to take the bull by the horns and wash his own sweatshirt. Seconds after he located and stepped into the laundry room, he shouted to his wife, "What setting do I use on the washing machine?"

"It depends," the wife replied. "What does it say on your shirt?"

The husband yelled back, "Dixie State University."

A young woman is on trial for bashing her husband with his guitars. The judge asks her, "First offender? (first a Fender)"

She replies, "No, your honor. First a Gibson, then a Fender."

A man asked his wife, "What would you do if I won the lottery?"

She replied, "I'd take half and leave you."

"Great," he said, "I won $12. Here's $6 ... stay in touch."

Cheryl treated her husband, Jim, by taking him to a strip club for his birthday. Entering the club, the doorman says, "Hi Jim. How are you?"

Cheryl asks, "How does he know you?"

Jim replies, "Oh, we were high school buddies."

Inside the bartender says, "The usual, Jim?"

Jim says to his wife, "Before you say anything, he's on my bowling team."

As they sit at a table, a stripper comes over and says, "Hi Jimmy. Do you want the special again?"

Cheryl grabbed Jim, stormed out of the club, and jumps into a taxi. The taxi driver says, "Hey Jimmy. You must be drunk because you surely picked an ugly one this time."

Jimmy had a nice funeral. Cheryl was found not guilty due to mental cruelty.

A guy is shopping at the local supermarket and notices a beautiful blonde who waves at him and says hello. He's surprised because he doesn't recognize her. He asks, "Do you know me?"

She replies, "I think you are the father of one of my kids."

He panics and thinks of the only time he was unfaithful to his wife. He blurts out, "OMG! Are you the woman I picked up in Joe's Bar years ago?"

The woman looks at him with wide eyes and responds, "No, I'm your son's math teacher."

Fred returned from a week long business trip exhausted and eager for a relaxing evening. Betty, his wife, greeted him and brought him a cool adult beverage.

"How was the trip?" Betty asked.

"Don't even ask," Fred said sipping his drink. He looked around the room, hoping to spot his dog.

"Where's Rover?" he inquired.

Betty took a deep breath, squared her shoulders, and said, "I'm sorry dear. Rover was in the street and was killed by a truck yesterday."

Fred leapt out of the chair, spilling his drink. "What ... what ..." he sputtered. "What kind of a way is that to tell me such bad news? Couldn't you soften it a little?

"How?" Betty asked.

"Well, I don't know," Fred replied. "Maybe prepared me for the bad news instead of just blurting it out. You could have said 'Rover was playing in the street with the neighbor kids. They were running and jumping, the kids laughing. Then out of nowhere a truck came barreling down the street barely missing the kids and hitting Rover.'"

"I guess you're right," Betty said apologetically. "I'm sorry. I was so upset that I didn't think much about how you would react."

Calmer now, Fred said, "That's all right. It's just a shock being told right out like that."

He sat back in his chair and sighed, "I think we should go out for dinner tonight. By the way, where's my mom?"

Betty hesitated and then said, "Well, she was playing in the street with the neighbor kids ..."

Alan and his wife Kathy were having an argument about who should brew the coffee each morning. Kathy said, "You should do it because you get up first, and then we don't have to wait as long to get our coffee."

Alan replied, "You're in charge of cooking around here, and you should do it because it is your job and I can wait for my coffee."

Kathy answers, "No, you should do it, and besides it's in the Bible that the man should brew the coffee."

Alan replies, "I don't believe that. Show me."

Kathy fetches the Bible and opened the New Testament and shows him the top of several pages that indeed says, "Hebrews. (he brews)"

Mrs. Smith is visiting her son, Anthony, for dinner. Anthony lives with a female roommate, Maria. During the meal, his mother couldn't help but notice how pretty Anthony's roommate is. Over the course of the evening, while watching the two interact, she started to wonder if there was more between Anthony and his roommate than meets the eye.

Reading his mom's thoughts, Anthony volunteered, "I know what you must be thinking, but I assure you, Maria and I are just roommates.'"

About a week later, Maria came to Anthony saying, "Ever since your mother came to dinner, I've been unable to find the silver sugar bowl. You don't suppose she took it, do you?"

"Well, I doubt it, but I'll contact her, just to be sure." So, he sat down and wrote an email:

Dear Mama,

I'm not saying that you "did" take the sugar bowl from my house; I'm not saying that you "did not" take it. But the fact remains that it has been missing ever since you were here for dinner.

Your Loving Son,

Anthony

A couple of days later, Anthony received an email reply from his mama which read:

Dear son,

I'm not saying that you "do" sleep with Maria, and I'm not saying that you "do not" sleep with her. But the fact remains that if she was sleeping in her OWN bed, she would have found the sugar bowl by now.

Your Loving Mama

———————

"Congratulations my boy!" said the groom's uncle. "I'm sure you'll look back and remember today as the happiest day of your life."

"But I'm not getting married until tomorrow," protested his nephew.

"I know," replied the uncle. "That's exactly what I mean."

———————

Chapter 12
Old People Jokes

One-Liners, Riddles, and Puns

At our age we can hide our own Easter Eggs, wait half an hour, and have no clue where we put them.

_____

Don't worry about old age, it doesn't last.

_____

Two old guys were sitting at a bar talking. One leans over to the other and whispered, "Did you know elks have sex 5 to 10 times a day?"
The other old guy replied, "Damn, and I just joined the moose."

_____

At my age, "getting lucky" means finding my car in the parking lot.

_____

One good thing about getting old is that kidnappers are not very interested in you.

_____

You know you're old when you enter your birth year on an online form and must spin down the column of years like you're on Wheel of Fortune.

_____

One good thing about getting old is that your secrets are safe with your friends, because they can't remember them either.

_____

As you get older, eventually you reach a point where you stop lying about your age. Instead you start bragging about it. I love to hear people say, "You don't look that old."

_____

One good thing about getting old is your supply of brain cells is down to a manageable size.

_____

One good thing about getting old is things you buy now won't wear out.

_____

One good thing about getting old is in a hostage situation you are most likely to be released first.

_____

The older I get, the fewer things seem worth waiting in line for.

_____

Stories

A police officer called the station on his cop radio. "I have an unusual situation here. An old lady just shot her husband for stepping on the floor she just mopped."

"Okay, that is unusual. Have you arrested the old woman?"

The police officer replied, "Hell no, the floor's still wet."

_____

Three old guys were talking about what their grandchildren would be saying about them in 50 years.

"I would like my grandchildren to say, 'He was successful in business,' declared the first man.

"Fifty years from now," said the second, "I want them to say, "He was a loyal family man."

The first guy asked the third, "So what do you want your grandkids to say about you in 50 years?"

"Me?" the third guy replied, "I want them to say, 'He certainly looks good for his age.'"

_____

An old guy has trouble hearing and goes to the audiologist for a hearing test. His hearing is shot, and he gets hearing aids. After a month, he meets for audiologist for a checkup.

The doctor says, "With the hearing aids, your hearing is perfect. Your family must be really pleased."

The old replies, "Oh, I'm in a funny situation now. I haven't told my family yet. I just sit and listen to their conversations which they think I can't hear. In a few weeks, I've changed my will three times."

_____

An old guy is hiking through the woods. He comes upon a strange looking frog in a lower branch of a tree. The frog looks at the old man and says, "I'm not really a frog. I'm a princess. Kiss me and I'll turn back into a princess."

The old man considers the proposal. Then pick up the frog and sticks it in his coat pocket.

As the frog is being put into the pocket, she says, "Aren't you going to kiss me so I'll become a princess?"

"Nope," the old man said. "I'm 80 years old, what am I going to do with a princess? I'd rather have a talking frog."

––––––––––––

A couple in their nineties were both having trouble remembering things. During a checkup, the doctor told them they were physically okay, but might want to write things down to help remember them.

Later that night, while watching TV, the old man gets up and asks, "Want anything while I'm in the kitchen?"

"Will you get me a bowl of ice cream?" his wife replies.

"Sure."

"I'd like some strawberries on top, too. Maybe you should write it down so you don't forget."

"Well, I can remember a bowl of ice cream with strawberries on top."

The wife then adds, "I'd also like some whipped cream. You're gonna forget, write it down."

Getting a little irritated, the husband says, "I don't need to write it down. Some ice cream with strawberries and whipped cream. Sheesh."

The old guy makes it to the kitchen and about 20 minutes later returns. He hands his wife a plate of bacon and eggs. She stares at the plate for a moment and then says, "Where's my toast?"

––––––––––––

Morris and his wife Esther went to the state fair every year, and every year Morris would say, "Esther, I'd like to ride in the helicopter"

Esther always replied, "I know Morris, but that helicopter ride is 50 dollars, and 50 dollars is 50 dollars."

Finally, while at the fair, Morris said, "Esther, I'm 85 years old. If I don't ride that helicopter this year I might never get another chance."

As usual, Esther replied, "Morris, that helicopter ride is 50 dollars and 50 dollars is 50 dollars."

The helicopter pilot overheard their discussion and said, "Folks, I'll make you a deal. I'll take both of you for a ride. If you can stay quiet for the entire ride and not say a word, I won't charge you. But if you say one word, it's 50 dollars."

Morris and Esther eagerly agreed and up they went. The pilot did all kinds of fancy maneuvers, but not a word was heard. He repeated the daredevil tricks, but still not a word.

When they landed, the pilot turned to Morris and said, "Wow! I did everything I could to get you to yell out, but you didn't. I'm impressed."

Morris replied, "Well, to tell you the truth, I almost said something when Esther fell out of the helicopter. But, you know, 50 dollars is 50 dollars."

It was a warmhearted funeral. The minister said many nice things about the deceased, emphasizing his many good deeds during a long life. He pointed out the surviving widow and how they had been married 52 years. The minister then asked if anyone else wanted to speak. A young man got up and approached the pulpit. He stopped and whispered to the widow, "Do you mind if I say a word?"

"No, young man. Go ahead," the old woman said.

The young man gets to the pulpit and faces the audience. He slowly looks around and clearly says, "Plethora." Then he walks away from the pulpit and down the aisle. As he passes the widow, she grabs his arm and tells him, "Thank you young man. That word means a lot to me."

Four old retired guys are walking down the street in St. George. They turn a corner and see a sign that says, Old Timers Bar—All Drinks $.50. They look at each other and then go in, thinking this is too good to be true.

The old bartender says in a loud voice, "Come on in gentlemen and let me pour one for you. What'll it be guys?"

There is a fully stocked bar, so each of the men order a martini. In no time the bartender serves up four perfect drinks and says, "That'll be $.50 each please."

The four guys stare at the bartender for a moment, then at each other. They can't believe their good luck.

They pay the $2, finish their martinis, and order another round. Again, four excellent martinis are produced and the bartender again asks for $2. They pay up and their curiosity peaks. They have each had two outstanding martinis for less than five dollars.

Finally, one of them asks, "How can you afford to serve great drinks for 50 cents apiece?"

"I'm a retired tailor from Phoenix," the bartender says, "and I always wanted to own a bar. Last year I won the state lottery with a jackpot of $125 million and decided to open this place. Every drink cost fifty cents. Wine liquor, beer, it's all the same."

"Wow! That's some story," one of the men says.

As the four of them sip their martinis, they can't help noticing seven other people at the end of the bar who don't have a drink in front of them and haven't ordered anything the whole time the four guys had been there.

Nodding at the seven at the end of the bar, one of the men asks the bartender, "What's with them?"

The bartender replies, "They're retired people from California. They're waiting for Happy Hour when drinks are half priced."

———————

Yesterday I was at Costco buying a large bag of Purina dog chow for my loyal pet, Spot the Wonder Dog. While I was waiting in the check-out line a woman behind me asked if I had a dog.

Because I'm retired and have little to do, I told her no, I didn't have a dog. I was starting the Purina diet again. I added that I probably shouldn't because I ended up in the hospital the last time on the diet. But I had lost 50 pounds before I awakened in the intensive care unit of the hospital.

I told her the Purina diet was a perfect diet. The way it worked was to load your pockets with the dog food nuggets and simply eat one or two every time you felt hungry. The food is nutritionally complete so it works well, and I was going to try it again. (At this point, nearly everyone in line was listening intently to my story.)

Horrified, the woman asked if I ended up in intensive care because the dog food poisoned me. I told her no. I ended up in intensive care because I stopped to pee on a fire hydrant and a car hit me.

I thought the guy behind her was going to have a heart attack he was laughing so hard.

Costco banned me from their store.

Better watch what you ask retired old people. We have all the time in the world to think of crazy things to say.

An 80 year old woman had just gotten married for the fourth time. The local newspaper heard about this and sent a reporter to interview her. The reporter asked about her life, what it felt like to be marrying again at 80, and her new husband's occupation.

"He's a funeral director," she answered.

"Interesting," the reporter said. He thought a bit and asked if she wouldn't mind telling him a little about her first three husbands.

She gathered her thoughts and said, "I first married a banker when I was in my 20s. Then I married a circus ringmaster in my 40s. My third husband, whom I married in my 60s was a preacher. And now at 80 I married a funeral director."

The reporter looked at her and asked why she married four men with such diverse careers.

She smiled and said, "I married one for the money, two for the show, three to get ready, and four to go."

A rich guy is near death and fretting that he can't take his money with him when he goes. So, he asks God if he can bring it with him. "Please, I've been good." After listening to this guy whine for seemingly forever, God gives in and says he can bring one suitcase full of anything he wants to heaven.

The rich guy decides gold is good everywhere, so he fills his suitcase with gold bricks. Soon enough the old guy dies and gets to the pearly gates. St. Peter says, "Hold it, no luggage allowed." The old guy tells St. Peter that in his case God made an exception. St. Peter should check with the boss. Peter checks, and sure enough, the old guy is allowed to bring in one suitcase.

St. Peter says, "I've been doing this a long time, and no one has ever brought anything with them. I'm curious to know what you brought."

The old guy proudly opens his suitcase. St. Peter looks in and bursts out laughing. "Pavement? You brought pavement?"

A young kid is visiting his grandparents. The kid is observant and asks his grandpa, "Grandpa, you and grandma have been married for 40 years and you still call her darling, beautiful, and honey. What's the secret?"

The old man replies, "I forgot her name about five years ago and I'm scared to ask her."

The doctor that had been seeing an 80 year old woman for most of her life finally retired. At her next checkup, the new doctor had her fill out a form that included all her medications. As the doctor looked through the list, his eyes grew wide as he realized grandma had a birth control prescription.

"Mrs. Smith, do you realize these are birth control pills?" he asked.

"Yes, they help me sleep at night."

"Mrs. Smith, I assure you there is nothing in birth control pills that could possible help you sleep."

The old lady reached out and patted the young doctor's knee, "Yes, dear, I know that. But every morning I grind up one pill and mix it in the glass of orange juice my 17 year old granddaughter drinks. Believe me, it definitely helps me sleep at night."

Mark took his 85 year old dad to the mall the other day to buy some shoes. They decided to grab a bite at the food court. Mark noticed his dad was watching a teenager sitting close to him. The teenager had multicolored spiked hair—green, red, orange, and blue. Dad kept staring and the teenager noticed.

When the teenager had enough, he sarcastically asked, "What's the matter old man, never done anything wild in your life?"

Knowing his dad, Mark quickly swallowed his food so he would not choke when his dad responded.

"Got drunk once and had sex with a peacock. I was just wondering if you were my son."

A retired guy, Fred, volunteers to entertain patients in nursing homes. He took his portable keyboard along, told some jokes, and sang some funny songs for the patients. When he finished, he said he hopes all the patients get better.

One old guy replied, "I hope you get better too."

_____

A distraught senior citizen phoned her doctor's office. "Is it true," she wanted to know, "that the medication you prescribed for me has to be taken for the rest of my life?"

"Yes, I'm afraid so," the doctor told her.

There was a moment of silence before the senior lady replied, "I'm wondering, then, just how serious is my condition because the prescription reads, 'No Refills.'"

_____

An old guy was on the operating awaiting surgery. He was insistent that his son, a renowned surgeon, perform the operation. As the old guy was about to receive the anesthesia, he asked to speak to his son. "Yes, dad, what is it? said the son.

"Don't be nervous son, Do your best. And just remember, if it doesn't go well, if something bad happens to me, your mother is going to come and live with you and your wife."

_____

An old guy is standing at the pearly gates and St. Peter tells him, "All you need to have done is one good deed and we will allow you to enter heaven."

The old man says, "No problem," as he recounts how he once stopped at an intersection and saw a motorcycle gang harassing a young woman.

He got out of his car, walked up to one of the bikers, who was about 6 feet, 5 inches tall and weighed at least 220 pounds. He told the biker that harassing a woman is a cowardly act and that he would not tolerate it.

Then the old guy said he reached up, yanked on the biker's nose ring, and kicked him in the groin.

St. Peter is frantically searching the man's life in his book and says, "I can't find that incident anywhere in your life. When did it happen?"

The old man looks at his watch and says, "Oh, about five minutes ago."

_____

Elmer, an old guy living in Florida, owned a large farm. Out back on the farm was a large pond/swimming hole the farmer had fixed up nicely with picnic tables, horseshoe pits, citrus trees, grapes, and blackberry bushes.

The old farmer decided to go down and check on the swimming hole, he hadn't been on that part of his property in a while. He grabbed a five gallon bucket in which to bring back some fruit. As he neared the pond, he heard shouting and laughter. He got closer and saw a bunch of young women skinny dipping in his swimming hole.

He coughed loudly and made the women aware of his presence. They all went to the deep end, and one of them shouted, "we're not coming out until you leave."

Elmer frowned and said, "I didn't come down here to watch you ladies swim naked." He held the bucket up high and said, "I'm here to feed the alligator."

For many older folks, Facebook is something of a mystery. This may help, try applying Facebook principles in the real world.

This one old guy did it—everyday, while walking around, he told tell passers-by what he ate for lunch, how he felt at that moment, what he did the night before, and what he plans to do. He showed anyone he met photos of his family, his dog, him gardening, standing in front of landmarks, generally doing what everyone does every day. He listened to their conversations, giving a "thumbs up" and telling them he "liked" them. It worked just like Facebook. The old guy already has four people following him around town: two police officers, a private investigator, and a psychiatrist.

Fred was bored with retirement and decided to get a job as a Walmart greeter. Two hours into his first day, an ugly woman (real ugly) came in with her two kids. She was swatting and swearing at them. Fred said, "Good morning, welcome to Walmart. Nice kids, are they twins?"

The mom answered, "Hell no, they ain't twins. The oldest one's nine and the other is seven. Why would you think they're twins? Are you blind or stupid?"

Ever the wit, Fred replied, "I'm neither blind nor stupid. I just couldn't believe someone slept with you twice. Have a good day and thank you for shopping at Walmart."

Fred's supervisor said he probably wasn't cut for this line of work.

An old guy was flying down the highway when he sees the dreaded red flashing lights in his rear view mirror. He pulls over to the side of the road. The cop walks up to the car and says, "Man, you were going fast, waaay too fast."

The old guy replies, "I was just trying to keep up with traffic."

The cop says, "There isn't any traffic."

The old guy responds, "I know, that's how far behind I am."

Bob was out working in his front yard when he was startled by a car crashing through his hedge and coming to a stop on his front lawn. He rushed to help an elderly lady driver out of the car and sat her down on a bench. Still amazed, Bob said, "You appear quite elderly to still be driving."

"Well, yes, I am," the old woman replied. "I'm 97 and I'm now old enough that I don't even need a driver's license anymore." She continued, "The last time I went to my doctor, he did a complete examination and asked if I had a driver's license. I told him yes and handed it to him. He took scissors out of a drawer, cut the license into pieces, and threw them into a trash can. He said, 'You won't be needing this anymore.' So, I thanked him and left."

A woman was walking down the street and noticed an old man rocking in a chair on his porch. "I couldn't help noticing how happy you look," she said. "What's your secret for a long, happy life?"

"I smoke two packs of cigarettes a day," he said. "I also drink a couple of quarts of whisky a week, eat fatty foods, and never exercise."

"That's amazing," the woman said. "How old are you?"

"Twenty-six," he said.

Chapter 13
Political Jokes

One-Liners, Riddles, and Puns

Do politicians ever tell the truth? Only when they call each other liars.

———————

President Barack Obama's poll numbers are so low now … the Kenyans are accusing him of being born in the United States.

———————

How are God and President Obama similar? Neither has a birth certificate.

———————

What's one advantage of electing a woman president of the US? We wouldn't have to pay her as much.

———————

How do you know when a liberal is really dead? His heart stops bleeding.

———————

Have you heard about McDonald's new Obama Value Meal? Order anything you want and the guy behind you must pay for it.
Conan O'Brien

———————

Leftists use statistics like a drunken man uses a lamppost—for support rather than illumination.

———————

Why do libertarians shun bag and instant teas, proclaiming the superiority of real loose-leaf teas? They believe in proper tea (property).

———————

The Supreme Court ruled against having a Nativity Scene in Washington, DC. But this wasn't for religious reasons. They couldn't find three wise men.

———————

What's the worst thing about massacring a thousand Chinese students? An hour later, you feel like massacring a thousand more.

———————

Libertarians are anarchists with money.

———————

Ninety-eight percent of the adults in this country are decent, hard-working Americans. It's the other lousy two percent that get all the publicity. But then—we elected them.
Lily Tomlin

———————

How many Republicans does it take to change a light bulb? Two—one to hold the gun and stand watch and the other to change the bulb.

———————

How many Libertarians does it take to change a light bulb? One—he already read the Constitution, knows he has the right to the light bulb he chooses, and it was purchased on the free market.

———————

How many Democrats does it take to change a light bulb? None. They'd rather sit in the dark and blame it on Trump.

———————

A nihilist, a socialist, and a neo-Marxist walk into a bar and sit at the bar. The bartender walks over, gives them a long look, and says, "Sorry, we don't sell alcohol to anyone under 21."

———————

A Libertarian is a conservative who has been busted for smoking pot.

———————

A Libertarian is a liberal who has learned economics.

———————

I don't know why death and taxes are always coupled. You only die once.

———————

What's the difference between baseball and politics? In baseball you're out if you are caught stealing.

———————

The label on my body wash said, "Use liberally." So, I stood in the shower screaming about Russian collusion.

———————

Did you hear they're building a library for the President Nixon papers? No admission charge—you must break in.

Republicans work hard because we can't all be on welfare.

What do you call a handcuffed politician? Trustworthy.

Why does California have the most corrupt politicians in the country while New Jersey has the most toxic waste sites? New Jersey got first choice.

Stories

Three surgeons were discussing who makes the best patients on which to operate. The first surgeon said, "Electricians are the best, everything inside is color coded."

The second surgeon replied, "No, I think librarians are the best. Everything in them is in alphabetical order."

"I disagree," said the third surgeon. "Politicians are the easiest to operate on. There's no guts, no heart, no brain, and no spine. Plus, the head and butt are interchangeable."

Two families move from Saudi Arabia to America. When they arrived the two fathers got to talking and made a bet to see, in a year's time, which family has become more Americanized.

Well, a year later they met again. The first dad says, "My son is playing baseball, I had breakfast at McDonalds, and I'm on my way to pick up a case of beer. How about you?"

The second dad replied, "Screw you towel head."

Democratic Vice President Joe Biden is out jogging one morning and notices a little boy on the corner with a box. Curious he runs over to the child and says, "What's in the box, kid?"

To which the little boy says, "Kittens, they're brand new kittens."

Biden laughs and says, "What kind of kittens are they?"

"Some are Democrats and some are Republicans," the child replies.

"Oh, that's cute," Biden says, chuckles, and jogs off.

A couple of days later Biden is running with his bipartisan buddy former President George W. Bush and he spies the same boy with his box just ahead. Joe says to George, "You gotta check this out," and they both jog over to the boy with the box.

Joe says, "Look in the box George, isn't that cute? Look at those little kittens. Hey kid tell my friend George what kind of kittens they are."

The boy replies, "They're Libertarians."

"Whoa!" Joe says, "I came by here the other day and you said they were Democrats and Republicans. What's up?"

"Well," the kid says, "Their eyes are open now."

An elderly man suffered a massive heart attack. His family drove wildly to get him to the emergency room. After what seemed like a very long wait, the ER doctor appeared wearing his scrubs and a long face. Sadly he said, "There's nothing we can do. I'm afraid grandpa is brain-dead, but his heart is still beating."

"Oh, dear God," cried his libertarian wife, her hands clasped against her cheeks with shock. "We never had a Democrat in the family before."

Santa Claus, the tooth fairy, an honest leftist Democrat, and an old drunk are walking down the street together when they simultaneously spot a hundred dollar bill. Who gets it?

The old drunk of course; the other three are mythological creatures.

A Soviet Communist Party official came up to a factory worker and said, "If you drank a shot of vodka could you still work?"

The worker replies, "I think I could."

Then the Communist Party official says, "If you drank five shots of vodka, could you still work?"

The worker chuckles and said, "Well, I'm here aren't I."

There are two novels that can change a bookish fourteen-year old's life: *The Lord of the Rings* and *Atlas Shrugged*. One is a childish fantasy that often engenders a lifelong obsession with its unbelievable heroes, leading to an

89

emotionally stunted, socially crippled adulthood, unable to deal with the real world. The other, of course, involves orcs.

If Noah had lived in the United States today the story may have gone something like this:

And the Lord spoke to Noah and said, "In one year, I am going to make it rain and cover the whole earth with water until all flesh is destroyed. But I want you to save the righteous people and two of every kind of living thing on earth. Therefore, I am commanding you to build an ark." In a flash of lightning, God delivered the specifications for an ark. In fear and trembling, Noah took the plans and agreed to build the ark. "Remember," said the Lord, "you must complete the ark and bring everything aboard in one year."

Exactly one year later, fierce storm clouds covered the earth and all the seas of the earth went into a tumult. The Lord saw that Noah was sitting in his front yard weeping. "Noah!" He shouted. "Where is the ark?"

"Lord, please forgive me," cried Noah. "I did my best, but there were big problems.

First, I had to get a permit for construction, and your plans did not meet the building codes. I had to hire an engineering firm and redraw the plans. Then I got into a fight with OSHA over whether the ark needed a sprinkler system and approved floatation devices. Then, my neighbor objected, claiming I was violating zoning ordinances by building the ark in my front yard, so I had to get a variance from the city planning commission.

Then, I had problems getting enough wood for the ark, because there was a ban on cutting trees to protect the Spotted Owl. I finally convinced the US Forest Service that I really needed the wood to save the owls. However, the Fish and Wildlife Service won't let me take the two owls.

The carpenters formed a union and went on strike. I had to negotiate a settlement with the National Labor Relations Board before anyone would pick up a saw or hammer. Now, I have 16 carpenters on the ark, but still no owls.

When I started rounding up the other animals, an animal rights group sued me. They objected to me taking only two of each kind aboard. This suit is pending.

Meanwhile, the EPA notified me that I could not complete the ark without filing an environmental impact statement on your proposed flood. They didn't take very kindly to the idea that they had no jurisdiction over the conduct of the Creator of the Universe.

Then, the Army Corps of Engineers demanded a map of the proposed flood plain. I sent them a globe.

Right now, I am trying to resolve a complaint filed with the Equal Employment Opportunity Commission that I am practicing discrimination by not taking atheists aboard.

The IRS has seized my assets, claiming that I'm building the ark in preparation to flee the country to avoid paying taxes. I just got a notice from the state that I owe them some kind of user tax and failed to register the ark as a 'recreational watercraft'.

And finally, the ACLU got the courts to issue an injunction against further construction of the ark, saying that since God is flooding the earth, it's a religious event, and, therefore unconstitutional. I really don't think I can finish the ark for another five or six years."

Noah waited. The sky began to clear, the sun began to shine, and the seas began to calm. A rainbow arched across the sky.

Noah looked up hopefully. "You mean you're not going to destroy the earth, Lord?"

"No," He said sadly. "I don't have to. The government already has.

First reporter: "The cult of statism members seem totally brainwashed, and still place their blind faith in a false savior offering hollow promises of hope and change."

Second reporter: "And that concludes our report from the White House."

A Republican, a Libertarian, and a Democrat are seated separately in a restaurant when a poor man walks in; unbeknownst to any of them, it is Jesus.

The Republican summons the waiter and asks him to serve the poor man the best food in the house and put it on his tab; the waiter does so. The Libertarian asks the waiter to please serve the poor man iced tea and to put it on his tab. The waiter does so. The Democrat then asks the waiter to bring the poor man pecan pie with ice cream and to put it on his tab.

When Jesus is finished eating, He goes over to the Republican and says, "I was hungry, and you gave me something to eat. Thank you. I see you are blind in one eye." And he touches the man's eye, and it is healed.

Jesus then goes over to the Libertarian and says, "I was thirsty, and you gave me something to drink. Thank you. I see you have a bad arm." And he touches the man's arm, and it is healed.

Then Jesus walks over to the Democrat. The Democrat moves far back from Jesus and exclaims, "Don't touch me!! I'm on 100% disability!"

A lawyer, a doctor and a politician are all applying to become government secret agents. They have passed all tests but the final one. All three are in a waiting room ready for their final test. First, the lawyer is given a gun and told to go into the room and execute the person sitting in the chair.

The lawyer goes into the room, and sees a little girl blindfolded in a chair. He leaves the room saying he could not shoot her. The lawyer is told he failed the test and cannot become a government secret agent.

Next the doctor is given a gun and is told to execute the person in the room. The doctor goes into the room, sees the little girl sitting in the chair blindfolded. He leaves the room saying he could not shoot her. The doctor is told he failed the test and cannot become a government secret agent.

Finally, the politician is given a gun and is told to execute the person in the room. The politician goes into the room and the people outside the room hear a gun shot. After this they hear a lot of rustling and banging. Eventually, the politician comes out and says, "someone put blanks in the gun, so I had to choke her to death."

While walking down the street one day Nancy Pelosi is tragically hit by a truck and dies. Her soul arrives in heaven and is met by St. Peter at the entrance. "Welcome to Heaven," says St. Peter.

"Before you settle in, it seems there is a problem. We seldom see a high official around these parts, you see, so we're not sure what to do with you."

"No problem, just let me in," says Nancy.

"Well, I'd like to, but I have orders from higher up. What we'll do is have you spend one day in Hell and one in Heaven. Then you can choose where to spend eternity."

"Really, I've made up my mind. I want to be in Heaven," says the Nancy.

"I'm sorry but we have our rules." And with that, St. Peter escorts her to the elevator and they go down, down, down to Hell. The doors open and Nancy finds herself in the middle of a green golf course. In the distance is a club house and standing in front of it are all her friends and other politicians who had worked with her, everyone is very happy and in evening dress. They run to greet Nancy, hug her, and reminisce about the good times they had while getting rich at expense of the people.

They play a friendly game of golf and then dine on lobster and caviar. Also present is the Devil, who really is a very friendly guy who has a good time dancing and telling jokes.

They are having such a good time that, before Nancy realizes it, it is time to go. Everyone gives her a big hug and waves while the elevator rises.

The elevator goes up, up, up and the door reopens on Heaven where St. Peter is waiting for Nancy.

"Now it's time to visit Heaven." So, 24 hours pass with Nancy joining a group of contented souls moving from cloud to cloud, playing the harp and singing. They have a good time and, before she realizes it, the 24 hours have gone by and St. Peter returns.

"Well then, you've spent a day in Hell and another in Heaven. Now choose your eternity."

Nancy reflects for a minute, then answers: "Well, I would never have said it, I mean Heaven has been delightful, but I think I would be better off in Hell."

So, Saint Peter escorts her to the elevator and she goes down, down, down to Hell. Now the doors of the elevator open and she is in the middle of a barren land covered with waste and garbage. He sees all her friends, dressed in rags, picking up the trash and putting it in black bags. The Devil comes over to Nancy and grins menacingly.

"I don't understand," stammers Nancy. "Yesterday I was here and there was a golf course and club and we ate lobster and caviar and danced and had a great time. Now all there is a wasteland full of garbage and my friends look miserable."

The Devil looks at Nancy, smiles and says, "Yesterday we were campaigning. Today you voted for us and this is the reality!"

Listening to Winston Churchill expound at length on his political opinions, Lady Astor grew more and more furious. Finally, unable to contain herself, she snapped, "Winston, if you were my husband, I'd put poison in your coffee."

"And if I were your husband," returned Churchill, "I'd drink it."

Three guys—a Democrat, a Republican and a Libertarian—were sitting in a bar talking. They began arguing about what really being famous would be like.

The Democrat defined it as being invited to the White House for a personal chat with the president.

"Nah", disagreed the Republican. "Real fame would be being at the White House chatting with the president when the hot line rings and the president won't take the call."

The Libertarian said they both had it wrong. "Fame," he declared. "is when you are in the Oval Office and the hot line rings, the president answers it, listens for a couple of seconds, and then hands you the phone and says, 'It's for you.'"

Ms. Humphries, the freshman economics teacher, asked her class, "Who can tell me what caused the American Revolution to break out?"

"Taxation," replied a student in the first row.

"Very good, Sherry." The teacher turned to a boy who hand was waving. "Yes, Andrew?"

"I have a question Ms. Humphries. How come they teach us that we won?"

A little boy, Jimmy, wanted $100 badly and prayed for two weeks and nothing happened. He then decided to write a letter to God requesting the $100.

When the postal authorities received the letter addressed to God, USA, they decided to send it to the president. The president read the letter and was so impressed and amused that he instructed his secretary to send the little boy a $5 bill, as this would appear to be a lot of money to a little boy.

Jimmy was delighted with the $5 and sat down to write a thank you note to God. He wrote: Dear God, Thank you very much for sending me the money. However, I noticed that for some reason you had to send it through Washington, DC and, as usual, those jerks took $95 of it.

The president is walking out of the White House and heading toward his limo when an assassin steps forward and aims a gun.

A Secret Service agent, new on the job, shouts, "Mickey Mouse!" This startles the would-be assassin and he is quickly captured.

Later, the Secret Service agent's supervisor take him aside and asks, "What the hell made you shout 'Mickey Mouse'?"

Blushing, the agent replies, "I got nervous. I meant to shout … Donald, duck (Donald Duck)!"

———————

A recent article in the *San Francisco Examiner* reported that Nancy Pelosi has sued Stanford Hospital, saying that "after her husband had surgery there, he lost all interest in sex."

A hospital spokesman replied, "Your husband was admitted for cataract surgery. All we did was improve his eyesight."

———————

A guy walks into a country bar with a shotgun in one hand and pulling a male buffalo with the other. He goes up to the bar and says, "I want some coffee."

The bartender says, "sure" and gets a cup of coffee.

The guy drinks the coffee, turns and blasts the buffalo with the shotgun causing parts of the animal to splatter everywhere, and then walks out.

The next day, the guy returns with his shotgun and another male buffalo. He again goes to the bar and asks for coffee. The bartender says, "Whoa … we're still cleaning up your mess from yesterday. What was that all about anyway?"

The guy smiles and says, "I'm in training to be a politician. Come in, drink some coffee, shoot the bull, leave a mess for others to clean up, and disappear for the rest of the day."

———————

A Harley rider was riding by the Washington, DC zoo when he sees a little girl leaning into the lion's cage. Suddenly, as her horrified parents watch, the lion grabs her by the collar of her jacket and tries to pull her inside the cage.

The biker jumps off his Harley, runs to the cage, and hits the lion squarely on the nose with a powerful punch.

Whimpering with pain and shaking his head, the lion jumps back letting go of the little girl. The biker scoops her up and delivers her to her stunned parents. The parents profusely thank the biker. A reporter has watched the entire event.

The reporter walks over to the biker and says, "Sir, the was the bravest thing I've ever seen."

The Harley rider replies, "Well, it was nothing really. The lion was behind bars. I just saw this little girl in danger and acted appropriately."

The reporter says, "I'll make sure this won't go unnoticed. I'm a journalist and tomorrow's paper will have this story on the front page. So, what do you do for a living and what is your political affiliation?"

The biker replies, "I'm a US Marine and a Republican."

The journalist leaves.

The following morning the biker buys the newspaper to see if it contains a story about his actions. On the front page, a headline reads, "US Marine Assaults African Immigrant and Steals His Lunch."

And that pretty much sums up the media's approach to news these days.

———————

A driver was stuck on a highway leading into Washington, DC. Nothing was moving. Suddenly a man knocks on the driver's window. The driver rolls down the window and asks, "What's going on?"

The man says, "Terrorists have kidnapped the entire US Congress and they're demanding a $100 million ransom. Otherwise, they're going to douse them with gasoline and set them on fire. Me and some other folks are going from car to car collecting donations."

"How much is everyone giving on average?" the driver asks.

The man replies, "Roughly a gallon."

———————

An Englishman, a Scotsman, an Irishman, a Latvian, a Turk, an Aussie, a German, a Honduran, an Egyptian, a Spaniard, a Japanese, a Mexican, a Russian, a Pole, a Swede, a Moroccan, a Nigerian, a Finn, a Bulgarian, an American, an Italian, a Libyan, an Ethiopian, an Israeli, a Saudi, and a Brazilian went to a popular nightclub and were waiting in line to get in.

The bouncer came up to them and said, "Sorry, I can't let you in without a Thai (tie)."

———————

The Pope and Hillary Clinton are on the same stage in Yankee Stadium in front of a huge crowd. The Pope leans toward Hillary and says, "Do you know that with one little wave of my hand I can make every person in this crowd go wild with joy. This joy will not be a momentary display, but will go deep into their hearts and they'll forever speak of this day and rejoice."

Hillary replied, "I seriously doubt that. With one little wave of your hand … Show me."

So, the Pope backhanded her and knocked her off the stage. The crowd roared and cheered wildly and there was happiness throughout the land.

A CNN reporter walks into a neighborhood tavern and is about to order a drink when he sees a guy at the end of the bar wearing a "Make America Great Again" hat. It didn't take an Einstein to know the guy was a Donald Trump supporter.

The CNN guy shouts to the bartender, loudly enough that everyone in the bar could hear, "drinks for everyone in here, bartender, except for that Trump supporter."

After the drinks were handed out, the Trump guy gives the CNN guy a big smile, waves at him, and says in an equally loud voice, "thank you!"

This infuriates the CNN reporter, so he once again loudly orders drinks for everyone except the guy wearing the Trump hat. As before, this doesn't seem to bother the Trump guy. He just continues to smile and again yells, "thank you!"

Again, the CNN guy again loudly orders drinks for everyone except the Trump guy. And again, the Trump supporter just smiles and yells back, "thank you!"

At this point, the aggravated CNN reporter asks the bartender, "What the hell is the matter with that Trump supporter? I've ordered three rounds of drinks for everyone in the bar but him and all the silly ass does is smile and thank me. Is he nuts?"

"Nope," replies the bartender. "He owns the place."

Chapter 14
Religious/God Jokes

One-Liners, Riddles, and Puns

What do you call a sleepwalking nun? A roamin'(Roman) Catholic.

_____

What did Buddha say to the hot dog vendor? Make me one with everything.

_____

What do you get when you cross and atheist with a Jehovah's Witness? Someone who knocks on your door for no apparent reason.
Comedian Guy Owen

_____

Did you hear about the Buddhist who refused Novocain during a root canal? He wanted to transcend dental medication (transcendental meditation).

_____

How do you turn regular water into holy water? Boil the hell out of it.

_____

Stories

One Sunday morning, a mother went to wake her son and tell him it was time to get ready for church. The son said, "I'm not going."

"Why not?" his mom asked.

"I'll give you two good reasons," he said, "First, they don't like me, and second, I don't like them."

His mother replied, "I'll give you two good reasons why you should go to church. One, you're 59 years old, and two, you're the pastor."

_____

A Jewish Rabbi and a Catholic Priest met at the town's annual fourth of July picnic. Old friends, they began their usual banter.

"This baked ham is really delicious," the priest teased the rabbi. "You really ought to try it. I know it's against your religion, but I can't understand why such a wonderful food should be forbidden. You don't know what you're missing. You haven't lived till you've tried Mrs. Heller's prized Virginia Baked Ham. Tell me Rabbi, when are you going to break down and try it?"

The rabbi looked at the priest with a big grin and said, "At your wedding."

_____

A nun walks into Mother Superior's office and plunks down into a chair. She lets out a sigh heavy with frustration.

"What troubles you Sister?" asked Mother Superior. "I thought this was the day you spent with your family?"

"It was," sighed the Sister. "And I went and played golf with my brother. He enjoys it and I was quite a talented golfer before devoting my life to God."

"I seem to recall that," Mother Superior agreed. "So, I take it your day of recreation was not relaxing?"

"Far from it," snorted the Sister. "In fact, I even took the Lord's name in vain today!"

"Goodness, Sister," gasped Mother Superior, astonished. "You must tell me about it."

"Well, we were on the fifth tee ...and this hole is a monster. A 540 yard par 5 with a nasty dogleg right and a hidden green. I hit the drive of my life, I creamed it. The sweetest swing I ever made."

"And the ball's flying straight and true, right along the line I wanted ... and it hits a bird in mid-flight."

"Oh my!" commiserated Mother Superior. "How unfortunate. But surely that didn't make you blaspheme, Sister."

"No, that wasn't it," admitted the Sister. "While I was trying to fathom what had happened, this squirrel runs out of the woods, grabs my ball, and runs off down the fairway."

"Oh, that would have made me blaspheme!" sympathized the Mother Superior.

"But I didn't, Mother," sobbed the Sister. "And I was so proud of myself. While I was pondering whether this was a sign from God, a hawk swoops out of the sky and grabs the squirrel who still has my ball clutched in his paws and flies off."

"So that's when you cursed," said Mother Superior with a knowing smile.

"Nope, that wasn't it either," cried the Sister, "because as the hawk started to fly out of sight, the squirrel began struggling and the hawk dropped him right on the green. My ball popped out of his paws and rolled to about 18 inches from the cup."

Mother Superior sat back in her chair, folded her arms across her chest, fixed the Sister with a baleful stare and said, "You missed the fucking putt, didn't you?"

An elderly woman walked into the local church. The usher greeted her at the door and helped her up the flight of stairs.

"Where would you like to sit?" he asked politely.

"The front row, please," she answered.

"You really don't want to do that," the usher said, "the Pastor is really boring."

"Do you happen to know who I am?" the woman inquired.

"No," he said.

"I'm the pastor's mother," she replied indignantly.

"Do you know who I am?" asked the usher.

"No," she said.

"Good," he answered.

A second grade teacher gave her class a "show and tell" assignment. Each student was instructed to bring an object that represented their religion to share with the class.

The next day, the teacher began the assignment. The first student got up in front of the class and said, "My name is Benjamin and I'm Jewish and this is the Star of David."

A second student went to the front of the class and said, "My name is Mary. I'm a Catholic and this is a rosary."

The third student got in front of the class and said, "My name is Tommy. I'm a Baptist and this is a casserole."

A priest, a minister, and a guru sat around discussing the best position for prayer, while a telephone repairman worked nearby.

"Kneeling is definitely the best position for praying," the priest said.

"No," said the minister. "I get the best results standing with my hands outstretched to Heaven."

"You're both wrong," the guru said. "The most effective prayer position is lying down on the floor."

The telephone repairman could contain himself no longer. "Hey fellas," he interrupted. "The best prayin' I ever did was when I was hanging upside down from a telephone pole."

A well-worn one dollar bill and a similarly distressed 20 dollar bill arrived at a Federal Reserve Bank to be retired. As they moved along a conveyor belt to be burned, they struck up a conversation.

The 20 dollar bill reminisced about its travels all over the country. "I had a pretty good life," the 20 proclaimed. "Why I've been to Las Vegas and Atlantic City, the finest best restaurants in New York, performances on Broadway, and even a cruise to the Caribbean."

"Wow!" said the one dollar bill. "You've really had an exciting life."

"So, tell me," said the 20, "where have you been throughout your life?"

The one dollar bill replies, "Oh, I've been to the Methodist Church, the Baptist Church, the Lutheran Church."

The 20 dollar bill interrupts, "What's a church?"

A young couple invited their elderly pastor for Sunday dinner. While the couple was in the kitchen preparing the meal, the pastor asked their son what they were having for dinner.

"Goat," the little boy answered.

"Goat?" replied the startled man of the cloth, "Are you sure about that?"

"Yep," said the youngster. "I heard dad say to mom, 'Today is just as good as any to have that old goat for dinner.'"

Mike was anxiously driving down the street because he had an important meeting and couldn't find a parking place.

Looking up to heaven, Mike said, "Lord take pity on me. If you find me a parking place, I will go to Mass every Sunday for the rest of my life and give up the Irish Whiskey!"

Miraculously, a parking place appeared.

Mike looked up again and said, "Never mind, I found one."

A Yankee (person from a northern state) was driving through a small southern town where there was a Nativity Scene, it was close to Christmas, that showed great skill and talent had gone into creating it. The Yankee noticed one small detail that baffled him—the three wise men were wearing firemen's helmets.

He stopped at a convenience store near the edge of town for gas and asked the woman behind the counter about the helmets.

She quickly became angry, "you damn Yankees never do read the Bible!"

The Yankee said he did read the Bible, but couldn't recall anything about firemen in the book.

The woman grabbed her Bible from beneath the counter and slammed it on the counter. She ruffled through some pages and finally jabbed her finger at a passage. Sticking the book in the Yankee's face she said, "The three wise men came from afar (a fire)."

An elderly woman owned a parrot—albeit a parrot with a bad habit. The parrot, named Mary, was female and about the only phrase it reliably said was, "I'm a swinger, I'm a swinger."

Finally, fed up with the bird, the old woman told her parish priest about the parrot. The priest, Father O'Hara, was amazed, "What a coincidence. I happen to own two parrots myself. Two male parrots named Matthew and Mark. They spend much of the day holding rosary beads in their feet and praying."

"Wow," the old woman exclaimed. "Could I bring Mary to your place to hang out with Matthew and Mark? Maybe she will learn some better phrases."

"Certainly," Father O'Hara said.

A few days later the old woman brought Mary the parrot to the Father's house. They placed Mary on a perch between the parrots Matthew and Mark. The birds bobbed their heads and examined each other. Then Mary said, "I'm a swinger."

Matthew and Mark looked at each other, and said at the same time, "Our prayers have been answered."

A preacher was completing a sermon on discipline and temperance. With much emotion he said, "If I had the power, I'd take all the beer in this town and throw all those bottles in the river. And I'd take all the wine and throw those bottles in the river." He was on a roll, and loudly exclaimed, "Then I'd take all the whisky and throw those bottles in the river. Amen."

The song leader then stood cautiously and announced with a smile, "For our closing song, let us sing Hymn #365, 'Shall We Gather at the River.'"

God was looking down at Earth and saw all the bad rascally behavior that was going on. He was not pleased and decided to send an angel to Earth to check things out.

The angel completed his mission and upon returning to heaven he reported to God, "Yes, it is bad on Earth. I'd estimate that 95% are misbehaving and only 5% are not."

God thought for a moment and said, "That's not good. I'd better send another angle to verify this data, get a second opinion."

A few days later the second angel returned and reported to the boss, "Yes, it is absolutely true. The earth is in a steep decline; 95% are misbehaving and only 5% are being good."

God was not pleased. He decided to email the 5% that were doing good. He wanted to encourage them and support their good behavior. Do you know what the email said? Just wondering, I didn't get one either.

A newly arrived soul was walking around heaven. The angel Gabriel is giving him a tour. They walk to a barn and Gabriel says, "We keep the holy cow in there. And over there in that lake is where we keep the holy mackerel." They keep walking and pass an outhouse. The newly arrived

103

soul gives the small structure a close look. Gabriel explains, "I guess I don't have to tell you what we keep in there."

One Sunday morning, the pastor noticed little Johnny standing in the foyer of the church staring at a large plaque. The plaque displayed a large list of names with small American flags mounted on either side of it.

The six-year old had stared at the plaque for some time, so the pastor walked up and stood by the little boy. "Good morning Johnny."

"Good morning, pastor," Johnny replied and pointed to the plaque. "Pastor, what is this?"

The pastor replied, "Well, son, it's a memorial to all the young men and women who died in the service."

They stood together, staring at the large plaque.

Finally, little Johnny, his voice barely audible and squeaking with fear, asked, "Which service, the 8:00 am or the 10:30 am?"

Michael, the pastor, decided to skip church one Sunday morning and go play golf instead. He told his assistant he wasn't feeling well and then drove to a golf course in another city so nobody would recognize him.

The first hole was a 350 yard monster. Michael teed off and a huge gust of wind caught his ball, carried it an extra hundred yards, and dropped it right in the hole—a 350 yard hole-in-one.

An angel looked at God and said, "Why did you do that?"

God chuckled and replied, "Who's he gonna tell?"

The monastery had strict rules about maintaining silence. The monks could speak once a year, and then for only a few minutes. On the appointed day, one young monk said, "I wish we could have seeds in our rye bread."

A year went by, and speaking day came around again. A different monk said, "I prefer rye bread without seeds."

The following year, a third monk remarked, "I just can't stand this constant bickering."

When the old man, Dave, got home he looked in the mirror and didn't like what he saw. "I'm going to live to be a 100."

He went on a strict diet, quit drinking and smoking, and began exercising every day. After a year, Dave looked younger than he had at 70.

One day he was out for his daily three mile walk. He stepped off the curb to cross the street and was hit by a car.

As he lay dying, Dave looked up at the sky and said, "God, how could you do this to me?"

A deep voice, which only Dave could hear, answered, "Sorry Dave, my bad. To tell the truth, I didn't recognize you."

God had been busy. He had created the heavens and earth, a bunch of plants and animals, and Adam and Eve. Adam and Eve were walking around and spied another person playing a guitar. Adam asked, "Who is that guy over there?" God replied, "That's Keith Richards. He was here before I arrived."

Chapter 15
Science/Technology Jokes

One-Liners, Riddles, and Puns

If you get cold inside a structure, just stand in the corner for a while. They're usually 90 degrees.

I'm reading a book about anti-gravity. I just can't put it down.

I stayed up all night to see where the sun went. Then it dawned on me.

Geology rocks, but geography is where it's at.

I was gonna tell a time travel joke, but you guys didn't get it.

What did the computer do at lunchtime? It had a byte (bite).

Why did the computer keep sneezing? It had a virus.

Why was the computer cold? Because it left its Windows open.

Two hydrogen atoms meet. One says, "I've lost my electron." The other says, "Are you sure?" The first replies, "Yes, I'm positive."

You know you're a bad driver when Siri says, "In 400 feet, stop and let me out."

There's a fine line between a numerator and a denominator. Only a fraction of people will find this funny. (A numerator is the number above the line in a common fraction showing how many of the parts indicated by the denominator are taken, for example, 2 in 2/3.)

When is the moon heaviest? When it is full.

_____

What is an astronaut's favorite key on a computer keyboard? The space bar.

_____

What is an astronaut's favorite candy bar? A Mars bar.

_____

What was the first animal in space? The cow that jumped over the moon.

_____

What's a tornado's favorite game? Twister.

_____

What do you call a fossil that doesn't want to work? Lazy bones.

_____

Stories

The world's first fully computerized airplane was ready for its maiden flight with passengers, but without pilots or crew. The plane automatically taxied to the boarding area and automatically opened the door. The passengers boarded and took their seats, all without human intervention.

The plane then moved to the runway and readied for takeoff. "Good afternoon ladies and gentlemen," a computerized voice intoned. "Welcome to the debut of the world's first fully computerized airplane. Everything on this plane is electronically controlled. Just sit back and relax. Nothing can go wrong ... Nothing can go wrong ... Nothing can go wrong ..."

_____

A father adopted a puppy from the local animal shelter to give to his son, his first dog. The boy asked what he should name the puppy. The father answered, "You can name him whatever you like, but be sure it's something you can remember. You'll be using it as a security question answer for the rest of your life."

_____

Chapter 16
Sports/Exercise Jokes

One-Liners, Riddles, and Puns

All the fat guys watch me and say to their wives, "See there's a fat guy doing okay. Bring me another beer."
Mickey Lolich, Detroit Tigers pitcher

My knees look like they lost a knife fight with a midget.
E. J. Holub, Kansas City Chiefs linebacker regarding his 12 knee operations

---

My theory is that if you can buy an ice cream cone and make it hit your mouth, you can learn to play. If you stick it on your forehead, your chances aren't as good.
Vic Braden, tennis instructor

What can you serve, but cannot eat? A tennis ball.

How do baseball players stay cool? They sit next to their fans.

Why is basketball such a messy sport? Because all the players dribble on the floor.

Why do golfers wear two pairs of pants? In case they get a hole in one.

Why is tennis such a loud sport? Because the players raise a racquet (racket).

When the doctors operated, I told them to put in a Koufax fastball. They did—but it was Mrs. Koufax's.
Tommy John, NY Yankees pitcher recalling his 1974 arm surgery

---

I don't exercise at all. If God had meant us to touch our toes, he would have put them further up our body.

The advantage of exercising every day is that you die healthier.

I joined the gym about six months ago and there is no progress in weight loss or toning up. Well, I'm going there in person tomorrow to find out what's really going on.

When I'm on the road, my greatest ambition is to get a standing boo.
Al Hrabosky, major league relief pitcher

The only difference between me and General Custer is that I have to watch game films on Sunday.
Rick Venturi, Northwestern University football coach

If you are going to try cross-country skiing, start with a small country.

Stories

Bob had 50 yard line tickets for the Super Bowl. As he sat down, he noticed the seat next to him was empty. He asked the old man on the other side of the empty seat whether anyone was sitting there.

"No," the man replied, "The seat is empty."

That's incredible," said Bob. "Who in right mind would have a seat on the 50 yard line for the Super Bowl and not use it?"

The old man replied, "Well, actually the seat belongs to me. I was supposed to come with my wife, but she passed away. This will be the first Super Bowl we haven't been together since we got married in 1980."

Bob said, "Oh, I'm sorry to hear that. That's terrible. But couldn't you find someone else—a friend or relative, or even a neighbor to use the seat?"

The old man shook his head, "No, they're all at the funeral."

Two old women, Rose and Jane, had been friends nearly all their lives. When it became clear Rose was dying, Jane visited her every day.

One day Jane said, "Rose, we both loved playing women's softball all our lives. Please do me one favor, when you get to Heaven, somehow let me know if there's women's softball there."

109

Rose looked up from her deathbed and said, "Jane, you've been my best friend for many years. If it is at all possible, I'll do this favor for you." Soon after that, Rose died.

A few nights later, Jane was awakened from a sound sleep by a flash of white light and a voice called out to her, "Jane, Jane."

"Who is it?" asked Jane.

"Jane, it's me, Rose."

"You're not Rose. Rose just died."

"I'm telling you, it's me, Rose," insisted the voice.

"Rose! Where are you?" Jane said.

"In Heaven," replied Rose. "I have some really good news and a little bad news."

"Tell me the good news first," said Jane.

"The good news," Rose said, "is that there is softball in Heaven. All our old buddies that died before me are here. We are all young again. The fields are great, and we never get rained out. Best if all, we can play softball as much as we want and never get tired."

"That's fantastic," said Jane. "So, what's the bad news?"

"You're pitching next Tuesday."

During his weekly golf match, Christopher stopped and turned to see a funeral procession driving slowly by on the road adjacent to the golf course. He took off his cap and stood silently while the cars went by. When the last car passed, he put his cap back on, and proceeded to sink a difficult putt.

"Congratulations," his opponent said. "I was sure the funeral procession was going to ruin your concentration."

"It was a close call," Christopher said. "After all, next month we would have been married for 25 years."

The guide was leading the hunting party deeper and deeper into the woods. Finally, he threw up his hands and sighed. "We're lost," he said.

One member of the hunting party yelled, "Lost? You said you were the best guide in all of Vermont."

"I am," the guide replied. "But we've been in Canada the last two hours."

——————

Chapter 17
Work/Jobs/Money Jokes

One-Liners, Riddles, and Puns

I think I want a job cleaning mirrors. It's something I could really see myself doing.

I'm working as hard as I can to get my life and money to run out at the same time. If I can just die after lunch on Tuesday, everything will be perfect. Doug Sanders, professional golfer

---

I've done some terrible things for money ... like getting up really early to go to work.

If money doesn't grow on trees, then why do banks have branches?

There was a safety meeting at work. The safety officer asked me, "What steps would you take in the event of a fire?" "Freaking big ones," was the wrong answer.

Did you hear about the cross-eyed teacher who lost her job? She couldn't control her pupils.

I asked my letter carrier why my letters were all wet. He said, "postage dew" (due).

At work, the boss gathered the employees and asked for two things we like most about our jobs. Apparently, lunch time and quitting time weren't the right answers.

John went to the bank and told the teller, "I would like to open a joint account."

The teller answered, "Okay, with whom?"

John replied, "Whoever has lots of money."

_____

Stories

Janice and her work computer seldom got along. One day while sitting at her workstation, the damn computer quit working. She knew what to do and called the tech support division.

The tech support guy got on the line and told Janice to right click on the screen.

"Okay," Janice said.

The tech support guy said, "Did you get a pop-up menu?"

Janice, "Nope."

The tech support guy says, "Okay, right click again. Now do you see a pop-up menu?"

Janice, "No, nothing has changed."

"Okay, Janice. Can you tell me what you have done to this point?"

Janice replied, "Sure. You told me to write (right) 'click' on the screen and I wrote 'click' on the screen."

_____

A guy goes to his bank to cash a $400 check. He tells the teller, a trainee teller, that he would like large bills. The teller gives him a strange look and says, "I sorry sir, but all the bills are the same size."

_____

Betty and Jane were in a bar having a drink and comparing notes on the difficulties of running a small business. "I started a new practice last year," Betty said. "I insist that each of my employees take at least a week off every three months."

"Why in the world would you do that?" Jane said.

"It's the best way I know of to learn which ones I can do without," Betty replied.

_____

Henry was an employee at a large warehouse. A new hire, Fred, didn't know much of anything about the job. Henry says he'll help. He goes to the boss and askes, "The new guy Fred needs training on the forklift. Can I train him?"

"Not without supervision (super vision)," replies the boss.

Henry answers, "I don't have that. But I think I have super hearing. Will that work?"

The guy drove home and trudged into his house. He looked haggard and his wife asked, "Rough day?"

"You bet it was," he groaned. "All the computers were down, and we had to think all day long."

Susan loved her husband, Frank. For many years he was the best waiter at a posh restaurant. Frank suddenly died and Susan was devastated.

About six months after his death, Susan went to a medium who promised she could contact the dead. Susan and the medium sat at a small table and began the séance. After a short time, Susan saw her husband standing in the corner dressed in his waiter's outfit.

"Frank," she cried. "Come over here and speak to me."

From the corner a shaky voice wailed, "I can't. It's not my table."

A little, withered old man walked into the office of a lumber company. He meets with the foreman and says, "I want a job as a lumberjack."

The foreman politely tried to talk him out of the idea. After all, he was old, small, and way too weak to fell trees. Undaunted, the old man took an axe and proceeded to chop down a tree in record time.

"That's astounding," the foreman said. "Where did you learn to fell trees like that?"

"Well," the old man said, "you've heard of the Sahara Forest?"

"You mean the Sahara Desert," the foreman replied.

"Sure, that's what it is called now," the old man said.

Although he was a trained meteorologist, Jones had a terrible record of forecasting for the local TV news program. He became something of a local joke when a newspaper began keeping a record of his predictions and showed he'd been wrong about 300 times in a single year. That kind of notoriety got Jones fired.

He moved to another part of the country and applied for a similar job. One of the questions on the job application asked why he left his previous position.

Jones wrote, "The climate didn't agree with me."

_____

Charlie walked into a real estate management office and told the agent, "I'm moving from that apartment you rented me last year. Do you know where I can buy a couple of hundred cockroaches?"

"Of course not," the agent said. "Why do you want to buy cockroaches?"

Charlie replied, "The lease says the apartment has to be in the same condition as when I moved in."

_____

Chapter 18
Young People Jokes

One-Liners, Riddles, and Puns

If a baby refuses to nap, is that considered resisting a rest (arrest)?

___

A four year old presented himself to his mom before going outside to play. She examined the child and said, "Your shoes are on the wrong feet."

The little boy looked down and said, "I don't have any other feet." Fair enough.

___

In the supermarket, I overheard two women talking about their children. One said, "having a teenager is like having a cat that only comes out to eat and hisses if you try to pet it."

___

Why did the boy eat his homework? Because his teacher said it was a piece of cake.

___

The worst part of spanking a disobedient child in the supermarket is having absolutely no idea whose child it is.

___

A mother tells her young son, "Eat your spinach. It will put color in your cheeks."

The son replies, "Who wants green cheeks?"

___

A young boy was horsing around in the library. The librarian confronted him and said, "Please be quiet. The people around you can't read."

"They can't?" the boy said. "Then what are they doing in the library?"

___

Stories

One night a teenage girl brings her new boyfriend home to meet her parents. They were appalled by his appearance: leather jacket, worn out pants, a bunch of tattoos, black heavy motorcycle boots, and a pierced nose.

Later, after the new boyfriend left, the parents talked to their daughter and the mom said, "Honey, he doesn't seem very nice."

"Oh please, mom," the daughter replied, "If he wasn't nice, why would he be doing 500 hours of community service?"

The third grade teacher asked Maria to go to the world map and find America. Maria points and says, "Here it is."

"Correct," said the teacher. "Now, class, who discovered America?"

The class replied, "Maria."

A science teacher conducted an experiment for his middle school class. Four worms were placed in four separate beakers. The first beaker contained beer, the second wine, the third whisky, and the fourth plain tap water.

The next day the teacher showed the results: the worm in the beer was dead, the worm in the wine was dead, the worm in the whisky was dead, and the fourth worm in water was alive and healthy.

The teacher asked the class, "What did we learn from this experiment?"

Smart ass Bobby raises his hand and shouts out, "Whoever drinks beer, wine, or whisky does not have worms."

The third grade teacher asked Bob, "How do you spell 'crocodile?'"

Bob slowly spells out, "krokadial."

The teacher says, "No, that's wrong."

Bob replies, "Maybe it is wrong, but you asked me how I spell it."

The four-year old girl stared at her grandfather for a long time. Then she asked, "Grandpa, were you on Noah's Ark?"

"Of course not," he answered, chuckling.

"Then how come you didn't drown?"

The seventh grade teacher asks Donald what is the chemical formula for water?

117

Donald replies, "H I J K L M N O."

"What are you talking about," the teacher asks.

Donald says, "Yesterday you said it was H to O. (H_2O)"

Two young boys, Bob and Dave, are spending the night at their grandparents the week before Christmas. At bedtime, the two boys knelt beside their beds to say their prayers. The youngest, Bob, begins praying at the top of his lungs, "I pray for a new bicycle ... I pray for a new I-Pad."

Dave, the older brother, leans over nudges Bob, and says, "Why are you shouting your prayers? God isn't deaf."

Bob replies, "No, but grandma is."

Two young boys were playing in the backyard of one kid's house. The first kid has a new puppy named Ginger. The second boy asks, "Does the puppy bite?"

The first boy replies, "Ginger doesn't bite, but sometimes Ginger snaps."

It's half time in the locker room for a kid's football game. Team is getting crushed. The coach is pissed.

"You guys certainly have the physical skills to win this game. You are as big and fast as your opponents. But, you are not thinking out there—missing tackles and blocking assignments, running the wrong pass patterns. Man! Are you all stupid?" the coach shouts.

"I'm going to give you a snap IQ test. Tommy (the quarterback), what is 2 plus 2?" The coach asks.

Tommy winces, makes faces, and finally says, "four."

Before the coach can say anything, another player jumps up and says, "Coach, give him another chance."

The teacher asks Little Debby, "You have five cats and someone wants two of them. How many cats do you have left?"

Little Debby, "Five."

"Okay," the teacher says, "Let's say someone forcefully takes two cats. How many cats do you have now?"

Little Debby replies, "Five cats and one dead body."

———————

Little Bobby attended a horse auction with his father, watching as his dad moved from horse to horse, running his hands up and down the horse's legs, rump, and chest.

After a few minutes little Bobby asked, "Dad, why are you doing that?"

"Because when I'm buying horses. I want to make sure they are healthy and in good shape before I buy."

Looking worried, little Bobby said, "Dad, I think the UPS guy wants to buy mom."

———————

The parents of a toddler were worried that she had never uttered a word. When she was two years old, they took her to a series of specialists for tests. No one found a thing wrong with her.

Time passed and the little girl still hadn't spoken. On the day before her fourth birthday, her father put a plate of chicken, mashed potatoes, and spinach in front of the little girl.

The child pushed the plate away and said, "I hate spinach."

The father was astounded. He got his wife from the kitchen and said to the child, "Tell mommy about the spinach."

"I hate spinach." The child repeated.

The parents were overjoyed, laughing, dancing around the little girl.

When they finally calmed down, the mother said, "We're so happy you can talk, honey. But why haven't you said anything before this?"

The child said, "Up till now, everything's been okay."

———————

"Daddy, where did I come from?" the seven-year old asked.

It was the moment for which her parents had carefully prepared. They took her into the living room and got out several books, charts, and pictures. They explained all they thought she should know about sexual attraction, affection, love, and reproduction. Then they sat back and smiled at the little girl.

119

"Does that answer your question? Her father asked.

"Not really," the little girl said. "My friend Marcia said she came from Dallas. I want to know where I came from."

————————

Little Bobby's mother died when he was young. His dad would often take him to the cemetery to visit his mom's grave. During one visit, Bobby walked around reading inscriptions on various headstones. After he'd read a sizable number, Bobby asked his father, "Where do they bury all the bad people."

————————

Other Books by Tom Garrison

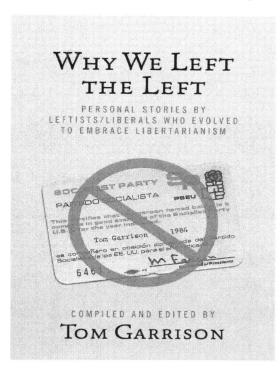

Why We Left the Left: Personal Stories by Leftists/ Liberals Who Evolved to Embrace Libertarianism (2012) examines a political question that intrigues almost everyone who studies, participates, or is interested in politics: "Why do people identify with a certain ideology and/or political party?" Numerous scholarly and popular books examine political ideology/party identification and why certain ideologies attract certain individuals. This book examines that question in two separate, yet joined phases. Why do people initially identify with the Left/liberalism and why do these same individuals abandon that ideology to evolve into libertarians? This inquiry is unique in its focus on 23 former liberals/leftists (including the author) who become libertarians.

One popular conception of libertarians is that they are, for the most part, disgruntled old white guys. While that group is represented, more than 25 percent of the stories are from women and more than two-thirds are by people younger than 50. This gender and generational diversity extends to occupations—contributors include college students, law students, an attorney, a professional artist, public school teachers, a chemist, writers, a filmmaker, a law professor, a stay-at-home mom, a firefighter, the CEO of a $40 million company, a TV reporter, an editor, the CEO of a free market environmental think tank, and a research engineer.

Why We Left the Left was awarded Honorable Mention in the non-fiction category of the League of Utah Writers Published Book Contest in September 2013.

Why We Left the Left can be found on Amazon at
https://www.amazon.com/Why-We-Left-Libertarianism-ebook/dp/B008H7HH0Y/ref=sr_1_1?s=digital-text&ie=UTF8&qid=1357702346&sr=1-1&keywords=why+we+left+the+left

Address all inquiries to Tom Garrison at: tomgarrison98@yahoo.com.
Consider visiting the *Why We Left the Left* Facebook page
https://www.facebook.com/pages/Why-We-Left-the-Left/173860626049768.

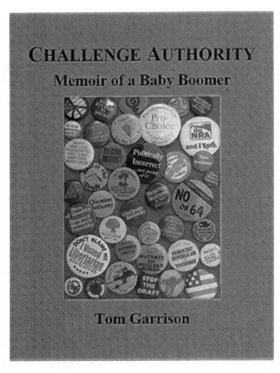

CHALLENGE AUTHORITY

Memoir of a Baby Boomer

Tom Garrison

Challenge Authority: Memoir of a Baby Boomer (2014) is about the Baby Boomer generation (about 75 million) which became politically active in the 1960s and 1970s, leaving its' mark on society. The sheer size of this human tsunami rolled through American society and fueled the Civil Rights, Gay Rights, and Women's Movements and agitation against war.

The 1960s mantra of "Challenge Authority" was the basis of the author's political activism. In a serious political context, challenging authority does not have to be negative, especially when done with a clear purpose. Challenging authority is a form of nonviolent action. You must know what you want to accomplish—hence the need for focus, confidence, and hard facts. A legal/ethical foundation is a prerequisite for such disciplined non-conformity.

Some of the 44 stories include: his challenging the Selective Service System (The Draft) for 2 ½ years during the Vietnam War era; being a war tax resister for many years; hosting an "Untying the Knot" party with his first wife after getting divorced; doing jail time (along with 1,959 others) for civil disobedience in trying to stop the opening of Diablo Canyon Nuclear Power Plant in California; twice running for Santa Barbara City Council in the mid-1980s as a socialist and being the only candidate (in both elections) to openly support gay and lesbian rights; and leaving the Left and becoming a libertarian in the mid-1990s. Of course, many of the stories are non-political: canal water skiing as a teenager; becoming a desert rat; and bungee jumping out of a hot air balloon on his 40th birthday.

Challenge Authority was awarded 2nd Place in the non-fiction category of the League of Utah Writers Published Book Contest in September 2014.

The print and ebook versions of *Challenge Authority* can be found on Amazon at https://www.amazon.com/Challenge-Authority-Memoir-Baby-Boomer/dp/1494798247/ref=tmm_pap_swatch_0?_encoding=UTF8&qid=1391118 276&sr=8-1

Address all inquiries to Tom Garrison at: tomgarrison98@yahoo.com. Consider visiting the *Challenge Authority* Facebook page. https://www.facebook.com/challengeauthority. Your comments are welcome.

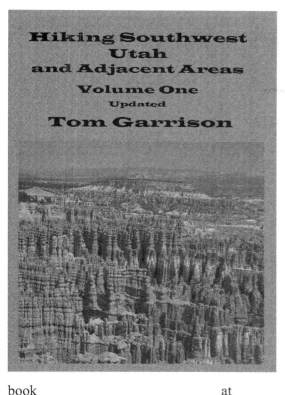

Hiking Southwest Utah and Adjacent Areas, Volume One, Updated is available in paperback. Each hike and all resource citations were updated in early 2018.

This guide is about hiking and generally exploring desert areas, specifically southwest Utah and adjacent areas (southern Nevada and northern Arizona). There is no better way to experience the ruggedness and beauty, the history of settlement by Native Americans and later pioneers, and the solitude than by simply hiking and exploring. The purpose in writing this book is to enhance the enjoyment of all who wish to sample the richness of southwest Utah and adjacent areas.

You can read the first few pages and purchase the updated book at Amazon.com: https://www.amazon.com/dp/1985347768/ref=sr_1_1?s=books&ie=UTF8&qid=1524000203&sr=1-1&keywords=hiking+southwest+utah+and+adjacent+areas+volume+one+updated

Included in the 141-page book are more than 25 color maps and more than 50 color photos taken during the hikes. (I took all the photos including the cover.) Twenty-five hikes are featured, each one includes: a map of the trail; a general description of the hike; trailhead access; average hiking time; hiking distance; fees and permits; elevations; best season for the hike; trail rating (difficulty); type of hike; United States Geological Survey map(s) used for the hike; online resources about each hike; a sense of humor/playfulness for each hike; and a full description of finding the trailhead and the hike.

Address all inquiries to Tom Garrison at: tomgarrison98@yahoo.com.

Consider visiting the *Hiking Southwest Utah and Adjacent Areas* Facebook page https://www.facebook.com/pages/Hiking-Southwest-Utah-and-Adjacent-Areas/1489605251309735. Your comments are welcome.

Hiking Southwest Utah
and Adjacent Areas, Volume Two
is available in paperback.

This guide is about hiking and generally exploring desert areas, specifically southwest Utah and adjacent areas (southern Nevada and northern Arizona). There is no better way to experience the ruggedness and beauty, the history of settlement by Native Americans and later pioneers, and the solitude than by simply hiking and exploring. The purpose in writing this book is to enhance the enjoyment of all who wish to sample the richness of southwest Utah and adjacent areas.

You can read the first few pages and purchase the book at Amazon.com:
https://www.amazon.com/Hiking-Southwest-Utah-Adjacent-Areas/dp/1533162107?ie=UTF8&*Version*=1&*entries*=0

Included in the 145-page book are more than 25 color maps and more than 50 color photos taken during the hikes. (I took all the photos including the cover.) Twenty-five hikes are featured, each one includes: a map of the trail; a general description of the hike; trailhead access; average hiking time; hiking distance; fees and permits; elevations; best season for the hike; trail rating (difficulty); type of hike; United States Geological Survey map(s) used for the hike; online resources about each hike; a sense of humor/playfulness for each hike; and a full description of finding the trailhead and the hike.

Hiking Southwest Utah and Adjacent Areas, Volume Two was awarded 2nd Place in the non-fiction category of the League of Utah Writers Published Book Contest in September 2016.

Address all inquiries to Tom Garrison at: tomgarrison98@yahoo.com.

Consider visiting the *Hiking Southwest Utah and Adjacent Areas* Facebook page https://www.facebook.com/pages/Hiking-Southwest-Utah-and-Adjacent-Areas/1489605251309735. Your comments are welcome.

Hiking
Southern
Nevada
Volume One

Tom Garrison

Hiking Southern Nevada, Volume One is available in paperback at Amazon.com.

This guide is about hiking and generally exploring desert areas, specifically southern Nevada. There is no better way to experience the ruggedness and beauty, the history of settlement by Native Americans and later pioneers, and the solitude than by simply hiking and exploring. The purpose in writing this book is to enhance the enjoyment of all who wish to sample the richness of southwest Utah and adjacent areas.

You can read the first few pages and purchase the book at Amazon.com:
https://www.amazon.com/Hiking-Southern-Nevada-One-Garrisno/dp/1986572153/ref=asap_bc?ie=UTF8

Included in the 150-page book are more than 25 color maps and more than 50 color photos taken during the hikes. (I took all the photos including the cover.) Twenty-five hikes are featured, each one includes: a general description of the hike; trailhead access; average hiking time; hiking distance; fees and permits; elevations; best season for the hike; trail rating (difficulty); type of hike; United States Geological Survey map(s) used for the hike; online resources about each hike; a sense of humor/playfulness for each hike; and a full description of finding the trailhead and the hike.

Hiking Southern Nevada was awarded 2nd Place in the non-fiction category of the League of Utah Writers Published Book Contest in August 2018.

Address all inquiries to Tom Garrison at: tomgarrison98@yahoo.com.

Consider visiting the *Hiking Southern Nevada* Facebook page at https://www.facebook.com/Hiking-Southern-Nevada-573183383051771/?ref=bookmarks. Your comments are welcome.

Made in the USA
San Bernardino, CA
21 February 2020

64781728R00078